A PLACE FOR ME

HELEN CAVANAGH

SCHOLASTIC BOOK SERVICES
New York Toronto London Auckland Sydney Tokyo

In memory of my father
WAPAA ALBERT HANNINEN
1905–1979

Cover Photo by Owen Brown

ISBN: 0-590-31765-2

12 11 10 9 8 7 6 5 4 3 2 1   10   1 2 3 4 5 6/8

A PLACE FOR ME

WILDFIRE TITLES
FROM SCHOLASTIC

Chapter 1

"**C**olleen, how old is your brother?" Shari Brubaker asked me during phys. ed.

"Which one?" I asked, and groaned inwardly. *Here we go again,* I thought. Now she'll say, 'Hey, listen, Colleen, since we're such good friends and all, how about inviting me over someday so I can meet him?' That's what other girls said when they made the connection: Rory Kelly/Colleen Kelly.

"He takes such great pictures," Shari said dreamily, and then rolled her eyes and leered like a maniac. "He can take *my* picture anytime!"

I had to laugh at her. Shari is about as subtle as red paint. I was laughing, too, because she didn't mean Rory at all. Wouldn't Patrick love to hear this? Up until now, it had always been Rory the girls raved about. Now it was Patrick. I can understand why, too, although even if they weren't my brothers they wouldn't be my type. Not at all.

"Patrick's too old for you, Shari. He's twenty,"

I said, adding, "Don't let him hear you say 'the one who takes the pictures.' Patrick's a photo-journalist."

Shari sighed and hiked up her gym shorts.

"Well, whatever," she said indignantly. "Anyway, he's very handsome. In fact, your whole family is. My mother met your mother at a council meeting and she told my father, 'That Maggie Kelly is a handsome woman.' "

She paused. "For her age, of course. How old *is* your mother, Colleen?"

My brother's age and now Mom's. No way. Shari and Mrs. Brubaker weren't going to get that out of me. I know Mom doesn't mind being forty-three, but I also know she doesn't want me broadcasting it to the world, or to Shari, which is practically the same thing. Shari and, I think, her mother, too, are the Rona Barretts of Springwood.

I lifted my shoulders in an I-don't-know shrug, and Shari let the age subject drop. She wasn't quite through with my family, though. She had to tell me how distinguished-looking Grandpa Shawn is, how gorgeous my sisters are.

"They're all just so . . . fascinating. What a great family, Colleen," she said in conclusion.

No. No conclusion yet.

"It's funny, though," she was saying now. "My mother and I can't figure you out. You're so different."

I was sure I had my face under control but maybe not, because suddenly Shari was all apologies.

"Oh, wait. I didn't mean . . ." She slapped her

own face. "Colleen, I didn't mean *bad* different. You're great-looking too, it's just that . . ."

I smiled and patted her shoulder. I knew what she meant.

"Don't worry about it, Shari," I said. "Every one says the same thing."

She looked relieved. Now she started all over again.

"Maybe someday after school, you'll invite me over, and you can just kind of casually introduce me to Patrick."

I laughed and moved up in the line waiting for turns at the parallel bars.

"Maybe," I said. "If you're a good girl."

Shari laughed, too, and then her face turned serious. "Sixteen isn't *that* young for twenty, is it, Colleen?"

Her big, brown puppy-dog eyes were hopeful.

"Maybe not," I said gently. "But I have a feeling Patrick would think so. He still treats me like his little baby sister."

"Ooooh," she said, and repeated the sound. "Ooooh."

But Shari recovers fast. "But that's *you*, Colleen. You're different."

Different. She was really throwing that word around a lot. Not that I haven't heard the word applied to me before. I've heard it, and I've thought it, too. Colleen Kelly doesn't really look like a Kelly, does she? She's kind of . . . *different*. It's the truth: I am. But if I don't look like a Kelly or act like one, then *who am I?*

Who am I? A boring question, I know. So

common. How many magazine articles and news-paper columns have been devoted to that prob-lem: Identity?

Anyway, whether I live up to the name or not, I am a Kelly — Colleen Marie Kelly — and at the moment I'm next in line for the parallel bars.

I can't be mad at Shari either. She doesn't mean any harm. How can you be mad at anyone who thinks your family is fascinating? They *are* outstanding, especially in a small town like Spring-wood, since Mom, Dad, and Grandpa Shawn own and publish the only newspaper:

"Everything under . . .
  THE SPRINGWOOD SUN"

It's a small weekly paper but good enough to win state and even national journalism awards. It's definitely a family business, and every mem-ber is involved in one way or another. Except for me. In this area too, I'm different.

Anyway, as a family, we have become fair game. Just like the contents of *The Sun*, we pass each week into "the public domain," which means people feel free to discuss us. Grandpa Shawn, who in his younger days used to be a foreign cor-respondent, as well as a columnist for *The New York Times,* says he doesn't mind it.

"Far better to be a big frog in a little pond," he said, "than a little frog in a big pond."

I think every one in my family really enjoys being local celebrities. It doesn't faze them at all. *Them,* I'm talking about, not *me.* Even in the tiny Springwood pond, I feel like a very tiny frog, maybe even a tadpole. So even if I do ask the boring question "Who am I?" I ask it silently. I don't want to be the only Kelly who doesn't know who I am or what I want to do with my life.

What also keeps me silent is that I like being silent. More than identity, my real problem is how to find the time and space to think about and find answers to my own questions. That's what I really need: a place and enough privacy so I can think deeply, read, dream, decide about things.

As it is now, from the time I get up in the morning until quite late at night, there are hundreds of things happening at home, at school, everywhere I go. People talking, radios and television sets adding their two cents — *noise*!

No one else in my family seems to need privacy or quiet time. They all think and dream and plan out loud. Dad likes to read the paper aloud to whoever is around, and Mom even talks as she writes her column.

All I can say is thank heavens for Samson. Samson is my big, beautiful, mannerly stallion. Samson may look like a brute because of his size, but he is very gentle, and I love it that he doesn't talk or ask questions or state an opinion. Samson and I share the peace and silence of Hagan's Woods, and it is when I am riding him that I sometimes come quite close to knowing who I am. But an hour or two every day isn't long enough to get to the other important questions of my life. The quiet time with Samson only makes the other times louder.

There is one more place where I can go sometimes to be quiet, and that is Grandpa Shawn's
room on the third floor of our house. Grandpa
Shawn is seventy-three now, pretty much retired
from journalism, although he often goes in to the
paper with Dad to "help out." He is always being
asked to lecture or to be master of ceremonies
somewhere. Usually, whenever I climb the stairs
to get away from it all, he's busy writing a speech
or his memoirs, or reading. Then sometimes he
takes a break, and we have an interesting conversation; but more often he'll barely look up from
his typewriter, and I am free to curl up in the old
blue wing chair, look out the window at the tops
of the maple trees, and just be.

I love Grandpa Shawn. More than anyone else
in this whole family, I think he understands me.
He doesn't seem to worry about me as, say, Mom
does.

She tells a story about me when I was a little
girl, and it's a story meant to point up the difference between me and her other four children.
Naturally, it's meant to be an amusing story, and
Mom certainly wouldn't tell it if she thought it
really bothered me. Anyway, her story begins:

"It was Colleen's fifth birthday, a beautiful Indian summer day. I was feeling rather strange, I
remember. Pleased because my last child would
be starting kindergarten, and I would have more
free time—and weepy because, after all, Colleen
was my last baby. Mixed emotions, you see . . ."

Mom never fails to wipe a tear from her eye at
this point, which is exactly what her readers do

week after week. Mom's weekly column in *The Sun* is the human interest kind, and her special writing talent is the ability to make people feel. Not so surprising. Mom *feels* almost constantly.

"It was her birthday! Sixteen other children at the party. We had a circus tent set in the backyard, a small merry-go-round we had rented, and a clown. There was a really fantastic cake and enough balloons to lift us all to the moon. Every kid there was in a state of bliss. And *where* was Colleen?"

Now she pauses a bit, and her voice gets a little catch in it.

"Colleen is in the *front* yard, under the plum tree, lying on her stomach, facedown in the grass. Well, I was *frantic*. She fell out of the tree, I thought, Colleen's hurt, my baby is hurt, or . . . worse.

"I knelt down beside her and put my hand on her back. Such a tiny thing really, such a curlyhead and so adorable in her white birthday dress with the red pockets shaped like hearts. 'Colleen,' I said . . ."

Now Mom rolls her eyes toward where we've been taught heaven is.

"Cool as a cucumber she rolls over and smiles at me. 'Guess what?' she says. 'Mommy, the grass is so beautiful and it *likes* me. Smell the grass, Mommy.'

"I didn't know what to say to her," Mom says. "Rory, Maureen, Patrick, Nora—they wouldn't have left the balloons, the cake, a real clown for . . . for *grass*! I knew then Colleen would be an unusual child, that she saw things the rest of us didn't see."

There is usually a short discussion then, ending with the decision: "Yes, Colleen is quite a special girl."

Of course, if I'm in the area, I get all kinds of fond glances and encouraging words about how wonderful it is to be "your own person," "unique," or a "real individual." What they *don't* say is, "Colleen, you don't seem to fit" or "Where on earth did you come from?"

That's one of the questions I try to think about with Samson or in Grandpa Shawn's room. Where *do* I fit in?

It's not that I think my family doesn't love me: I *know* they do. But I also know I confuse them, make them uneasy.

But really, they drive *me* crazy sometimes. There are days and nights when I wonder how much longer I can stand this family, this big, cheerful, chattering, competitive, captivating clan.

Chapter 2

"Trilig. Mish. Gaarg."

The voice was very loud in the darkness: a strange voice, growly. I jerked awake, stared holes in the blackness around me, and listened hard. Who? What?

"Pato. Steen. Bolik . . . mishhh!"

"Oh, be quiet, Nora. We're trying to sleep."

Maureen's voice was full of sleep, too full to sound very angry. But her voice made it all clear for me, made it safe, brought back the bedroom.

It was only Nora. Talking in her sleep again. The same old gibberish — Nora's Nightly Noises.

I exhaled, uncurled my toes and for the thousandth time yearned for my own room. My own room would solve all my problems; it would be perfect, the zenith (Patrick's favorite word). Right now it's impossible. Our house on Cloverdale Road has only four bedrooms including the one on the third floor. Which means Mom and Dad have one, Rory and Patrick share, and

Maureen, Nora, and I share. Share? Sometimes I wonder. I'll give you an example.

SCENE: Bedroom, second floor (turn right at the top of the stairs). A large, airy room with six (count 'em) windows. Three twin beds with dust ruffles and matching quilts in earth colors (Maureen and Nora's favorites). Three matching dressers, traditional in style, mahogany (the exact shade of Maureen's hair), a long library table bought at the Englishtown auction (Desk for Three Daughters), three chairs. Accessories include an electric typewriter, a pole lamp, a cassette recorder, a portable TV, AM-FM radio, floor to ceiling mirror, ballet barre, an easel with painting-in-progress, a sand candle (mine) a small bookcase (mine) a large bookcase (theirs), clothes, floppy hats, shoes, costumes, underwear, a belt rack, stacks of mail, and typing paper (all theirs), and a framed photo of Samson (mine).

TIME: Pre-dinnertime, about six P.M.

MAUREEN (frantic): Colleen, please put down that book for a minute and help me. I *mean* it. I want your honest opinion. Does this skirt make me look fat? Is my stomach sticking out too much? Don't lie. It's going to look even worse after dinner.

COLLEEN: You look fine, Mo. I mean it, you really look nice. Your stomach is flat as a board.

MAUREEN (plopping down on Colleen's bed, one

hand clapped to her forehead): Colleen! Why are you compelled to say the nice thing? You know you can't always do that. A day will come when you'll have to confront yourself. Now put down that book and tell me the real truth.

COLLEEN (removing her finger from the book where she has been hopefully marking her place): I *am* telling the truth, Maureen, you look beautiful. Your stomach is fine.

MAUREEN (rising from the bed, flouncing away angrily): Colleen, be true to yourself. Why must you always be so meek?

COLLEEN (hopelessly): But you *do* look beautiful, Mo.

MAUREEN: I know I do, but you shouldn't be afraid to disagree. I won't bite — I'm your sister!

I'm being sarcastic again, and I suppose I'm exaggerating but not much. It's really quite a typical scene, not just before dinner, but all the time. Just opening a book and being quiet and mild-mannered I can bring out all their worst instincts.

Nora is always trying to drag me along with her to her play rehearsal, or when she's covering the town council meeting for *The Sun*. Her main purpose is to teach me to be more outgoing and worldly, and ultimately to fix me up.

"Come with me today, Colleen," she'll say,

"and I'll introduce you to Ronnie Redman. He's playing the younger brother and he's darling. Too young for me, but just right for you. Colleen?"

I make some excuse. I know Ronnie Redman will not be right for me. Nora's taste in boys is not my taste. And I don't want to be fixed up.

Still, Nora is not quite as bad as Maureen. At least Nora doesn't nag at me all the time. I can never make Maureen believe that I really enjoy sitting quietly with a book, or without a book; that I'm not unhappy or depressed because I'm not joining in every conversation. Actually, this whole family (except Grandpa Shawn) seems to think alone means lonely, *unhappy* lonely. So far I haven't had a chance to find out about lonely. But I do know that alone is what I need and can't get enough of.

For instance, last night, even my biggest supporter, my kind, funny grandfather, put me on the spot. As usual, like everyone else, he didn't mean any harm.

We were all sitting at our huge round oak table having dinner and it was same kind of mealtime we always have; everyone eager to tell his or her "news of the day," giving and receiving advice: opinion hour, update time. In other words, a whole lot of talking going on.

For me, it was a tense time as the voices grew shrill. I can't help it — loud noises actually give me the shivers the way fingernails scraping against a blackboard do. I guess Rory has a good point when he calls me "Little Mimosa" and says, "In the world of trees, the mimosa is the shy one, shrinking away, flinching when anyone comes too close or touches her leaves."

Rory is a good reporter, or journalist, as he prefers to be called. In just two years of writing full-time for *The Sun*, he has earned some pretty prestigious awards. His articles are usually the hard-hitting, courageous, no-nonsense type. But when he says things like that, I know he's a poet, too.

Girls are crazy about him; guys too. They look up to him, and it's not just because he's six-foot-five.

Anyway, there we all were at dinner, all the Knights and Ladies of Kelly Castle, sitting at the round table. They were deep in conversation, which always comes second to food. My mind was wandering.

Suddenly, Grandpa was speaking to me. "A penny for your thoughts, Collie, darlin'."

Collie is the name Grandpa Shawn calls me, no one else.

It goes way back to when I was very small, and he used to hold me on his lap in the blue wing chair and read to me in the evening before I went to bed. I can remember the smell of wool, and pipe smoke, and the way he hugged me just before I climbed down from his lap. He would say my name in that special singsong voice, and when he did, I knew — I felt — I was deeply loved.

So now when he offered me a penny for my thoughts and called me by my special name, I couldn't get too mad at him. Annoyed at the intrusion but not mad.

"If I told you my thoughts, if I sold you my thoughts, then they wouldn't be my thoughts anymore, would they?" I said calmly.

I was careful not to speak rudely, but I meant every word. I know I have to share a bedroom, I know it's necessary to participate in most family activities (just because I am a member of the family), and I know I owe them all a lot as far as love and loyalty goes. I know all that, and as hard as it gets sometimes, I really try not to be difficult. But do I really owe them my thoughts? My insides? I don't think so.

Grandpa Shawn's silvery head nodded agreeably. "You've got a good point there, Collie," he said. "And forgive me — your thoughts would be worth much more than a penny."

Rory seemed to like my answer, too. He was smiling, a sly, foxy smile.

"And you wonder why I call her Little Mimosa," he said, sighing. "But you're right, Colleen — you're entitled. The rest of us, we don't sell our thoughts, we give them away. Whether anyone wants them or not."

There was something wistful in his voice when he said that, and for an instant I wondered if he ever felt overwhelmed by the family, too. Anyway, I hadn't meant to sound superior.

I saw Nora looking at me, a soft look in her eyes, as if she too had just caught a glimpse of the real me. But then she turned to Maureen and gave her a nudge.

"Where do you suppose we got her?" she said teasingly.

Maureen shrugged and flashed the smile that had almost won her the Miss New Jersey title two years ago.

"Maybe the Little People smuggled her in. Maybe she's royalty, Queen of the Leprechauns, maybe she's not a Kelly at all."

She winked at me, and I managed a smile. Inwardly, though, I was counting all my names, all the identities other people had given me: Little Mimosa, Collie, Queen of the Leprechauns, and my own thought, Beth from *Little Women*. No wonder I haven't been able to figure out who I am.

I knew that they weren't being critical, nor did they mean to hurt my feelings, but all I could think of now were Maureen's words: ". . . she's not a Kelly at all."

It bothers me because I *am* different. I *look* different. My family is made up of such colorful people. All seven warm-skinned and blue-eyed with dark red hair the color of polished mahogany; thick, wavy hair, shiny-beautiful. All except Grandpa Shawn. His hair is still thick but no longer Kelly-red. Now it's an elegant, silvery white. Privately I think of him as the Silver Fox and the rest of the family as the Red Foxes.

My own hair is a duller shade, not red, not blond, but somewhere in between. Mom says my hair is "topaz," but that's typical. Mom's a romantic; she'll choose the exotic word every time. I think my hair is more the color of toast, plain old ordinary toast. And my eyes are gray. Nice eyes,

large and wide-set like Shari said, but . . . gray.
Why do they have to be gray?

To make matters worse, my features are completely different from everyone else's, and although I'm as tall as my sisters, my bones are smaller. I have a short, straight nose, not the cheerful, cute, upturned kind the rest of them have. They all look strong and vital, and although I am just as healthy, somehow, next to them, I look fragile and, I think, rather washed out. A watercolor in a gallery of oil paintings.

I don't hate my looks. I really don't feel ugly or anything like that. I just don't like being the odd one, the misfit. I don't always feel so woe-is-me, but there are times, like now, when I feel on the verge of screaming.

But I never scream. Mimosa trees flinch, but they don't scream, and sweet little Beth from *Little Women* wouldn't have dreamed of raising her voice. She was an angel.

No one can accuse me of being *that* — an angel. Or they couldn't if they could read my mind sometimes.

Chapter 3

*S*amson would save me. If I hurried, I could still get an hour of riding in before dark and before I had to start my homework.

After-dinner cleanup doesn't take long. We all pitch in — teamwork. The system began long ago when Mom began to spend longer hours at *The Sun*, and when Mrs. Wheatley, our housekeeper, said she couldn't stay a minute past six o'clock. Mom explained it to us: "After all, Mrs. Wheatley has a family of her own." Later, I learned Mrs. Wheatley's real reason for the six o'clock deadline. Mrs. Wheatley is a Bingo freak. She goes to Bingo every night of the week.

Anyway, once the kitchen and dining room were shipshape, I ran up the stairs to my (our) room, changed my slacks for jeans and my shoes for riding boots. I grabbed a pullover sweater and knotted the sleeves around my neck. Hairbrushing and lipstick weren't necessary; Samson loves me no matter how I look.

"Going riding," I said to the living room in general.

No one heard me. They were all too busy talking.

"Riding Samson now," I said, straining my vocal cords.

Mom looked up and smiled. "That's nice, dear. Be careful. And as I was saying, Brian, I think that editorial about vandalism in the schools could be a lot stronger."

Except for the muted sound of a neighbor's stereo, it was a beautiful evening, with the hushed stillness of a church on Monday. It was the end of September, and Indian summer was definitely on its way out, too. It was chilly. Still, I didn't bother to put on my sweater; I didn't want to waste a second. Just the sight of my Samson, so solid and patient and strong, would calm me down, and the seething frustrations of this day would disappear. I bless the day Grandpa Shawn said he was mine, all mine.

"I know you will take good care of him," Grandpa Shawn had said on my fourteenth birthday. Then he added, in a very serious voice, "And I think he will take good care of you, too."

I board Samson at the Hagans' because, for one thing, our neighborhood isn't zoned for livestock. Besides, even if it was, I couldn't keep Samson at home. It wouldn't be fair to him. Our property is fairly large; large enough for a badminton court, a swimming pool, and two huge picnic tables (not to mention Dad's annual vegetable garden). A dog might be able to find enough space but not a horse. Not my mighty Samson.

Walking to the Hagans' from my house takes about five minutes, but tonight I was really hurrying, so it took about three. I was glad I hadn't put on my sweater.

Mrs. Hagan and her youngest boy, J. J., were in the yard outside the barn. When they saw me Mrs. Hagan waved, and J. J. hustled into the barn. As I approached, he stuck his head back out the door and said brightly, "I'll saddle up Samson for you, okay?"

I thought about it for just a second. Usually I enjoyed that part of it, too, but tonight I needed all the riding time I could get, and I knew J. J. was quicker at it than I was.

"Thanks, J. J.," I said. "I appreciate it." J. J. Hagan isn't more than eleven years old, but I always think of him as older because he's so serious. If it weren't for his straw-colored hair and dimples, I would have said, "Thank you, sir."

When J. J. returned a few minutes later with Samson, he was leading another horse, too. From the looks of her — slim, sleek, a proud head, slightly skittish, I decided she had to be a Thoroughbred.

"Beautiful," I breathed admiringly. "When did you get her?"

The horse's coat reminded me of black satin. If a horse can be glamorous, then this one was glamorous.

J. J. grinned. "She's an aristocrat," he said,

leaning his tanned cheek against the horse's belly, his eyes closing briefly. "My Dad said that."

His expression was suddenly very earnest. "Samson's a beauty, too," he said quickly, and then amended it. "Handsome, I mean."

The warm spot I have in my heart for J. J. Hagan got warmer. *He isn't just polite,* I thought, *he's kind.*

"Thanks, J. J., and for getting him ready for me, too. I can't wait; I'm just dying to ride him tonight."

I took Samson's reins and led him away from the black beauty for our few moments of private talk. I always talk to Samson before I mount him. In a way, I guess, I ask his permission, inquire how he's feeling. Not real talk but soft, murmuring sounds we both understand.

When I was mounted and ready to go, I took one last look at the "aristocrat."

"What's her name?" I asked.

"Black Satin." Mrs. Hagan and J. J. said it at the same time, and we all laughed.

"I thought it had to be," I said. "When I saw her, I thought of black satin."

"I thought, or I tried to think of more interesting names." A clear, deep voice had come from the interior of the barn, and I twisted around in the saddle, startled. It wasn't Mr. Hagan's voice.

"But black satin she was, so I figured Black Satin she had to be. Not very original, though."

Then from the dimness of the barn the owner of the voice appeared and leaned against the barn door.

"It's just as I remembered, Mrs. Hagan," he said, smiling rather shyly. "Except it's smaller, I think. The barn seems smaller."

There was a note of wonder in his voice and Mrs. Hagan laughed merrily. "The barn isn't smaller, Jonathan, you just got bigger. You've changed, not this old place."

While they chatted, I had a chance to look at him, although I tried not to make it too obvious. I took advantage of the fact that he was squinting, a sure sign that his eyes hadn't fully adjusted to the light of the setting sun after the gloomy barn light. If I was right, then he still couldn't see me too well.

He was tall with dark hair and a deep tan, his teeth very white against the darkness of his skin. His face was narrow, and his nose was the thin kind, too. Along with his narrowed eyes, he could have been almost cruel-looking, but nice full lips and thick dark eyebrows that tilted up at the corners saved him from that, made him definitely okay.

For one fleeting instant I had the feeling that I had seen him before and then, as he crossed the yard and stood beside Black Satin, I knew why.

The boy and the horse are just alike, I thought. My first impressions of the horse — "a beauty, a Thoroughbred, glamorous" — seemed to fit the boy as well. Like J. J., I quickly amended "beautiful" to "handsome."

And yet his glamour was not the flashy kind. His leanness, the way he held his head, the easy graceful stride as he crossed the barnyard made that other word seem right too — "aristocrat."

Suddenly, in my mind, appeared a quick series of what I recognized as book covers, Maureen's collection of paperback romances. *This boy could be the hero of every one of those books,* I thought. Only his name would be Brett or Bram, and he would be wearing a white silk shirt with long full sleeves. The shirt would be open to the waist. . .

Then I caught myself. And I accuse Mom of being a romantic?

". . . Colleen Kelly and Samson."

I realized Mrs. Hagan was trying to introduce us. I sat up straighter and managed a smile, although suddenly I was very self-conscious. Why hadn't I taken the time to brush my hair and do my face? Even a tiny dab of lipstick and blusher would have helped.

"Meet Jonathan Holmes. You already met Black Satin. Jonathan was born in Springwood," Mrs. Hagan said. "Started school here and was my first customer. He kept his pony here. He left Springwood about ten years ago, or was it eleven, Jonathan? He went abroad." Mrs. Hagan dragged out the last word and rolled her eyes. "Jonathan is a world traveler — a true man of the world."

He smiled again, a little embarrassed now. "Eleven years ago, Mrs. Hagan. I was seven. And I don't think boarding schools in London and Switzerland make me exactly a world traveler. Actually, I missed Springwood a lot." He made a sweeping gesture with one hand. "I missed this."

Now he looked directly at me, and for the first

time I saw the color of his eyes. Gray. His eyes were gray like mine.

"The countries I've lived in were nice," he explained, "but I'm very happy to be back."

The white and gray of his eyes were clear in contrast to the sun-darkened skin around them. I gazed back at him almost helplessly. I had the strangest feeling that he was saying something only for me. "I'm very happy to be back . . . now that I've met you."

Except, of course, that was plain stupid. He had just met me. Not more than five minutes had passed. Why would he . . .

He took a few steps until he stood beside Samson, close enough so that if I reached down, I could touch the dark smoothness of his hair, hair that I imagined was almost as satiny as his horse's.

"Fantastic horse," he said, stroking Samson's side with a touch that showed he loved horses.

He was silent for a moment, his head bent slightly. Then he looked up and smiled at me. It was a hesitant smile, though, almost bashful, and although I knew now he was eighteen he seemed much younger at that moment.

"Would you mind a riding companion? I hoped to get some time in tonight."

Now he threw back his head and laughed and just like that he'd lost any traces of shyness. "Mrs. Hagan, would you ask this nice girl if she would be my guide? I'm afraid I'll get lost. I've probably forgotten . . ."

"Go on with you, Jonathan. When you were five you knew the woods better than I do now. I clearly remember telling your mother: Never worry your head about Jonathan."

Mrs. Hagan came over to stand beside us and pretended to speak to me confidentially. "Maybe you better worry *your* head. Any boy who is so devious, who attempts to gain your sympathy . . ."

She hugged Jonathan suddenly and easily. He hugged her back. "Glad to have you back, dear," she said, and I thought I heard a little choking sound in her voice. I wasn't really surprised. Mrs. Hagan's first love may be horses, but she has a great fondness for two-legged creatures, too.

At that moment I caught a glimpse of J. J. standing in the open barn doorway. There was a funny look on his face, but when he saw me looking at him, he ducked his head. But not before I saw the knowing smile, the glint in his eyes. *Why, that little devil*, I thought. *He's watching this whole scene and he thinks he's got it all figured out*. After I said I was "dying" to be off riding tonight, here I was still lingering, because of Jonathan.

I could read J. J.'s mind ". . . because she's all impressed . . . because she likes him. Hmmmmm."

I couldn't blame him. Isn't that how I had been acting? All dreamy-eyed and breathless? Since when had any boy, any person, been more important than my need for some quiet time with Samson? Hagan's Woods was still almost the only quiet place left to me. And now was I going to let some boy change that? No way.

My mind made up, I carefully eased Samson

away from Mrs. Hagan and Jonathan. I could feel them both looking at me.

I didn't actually turn to look at them, but I said, very plainly, "It's going to be dark very soon. I better go now."

And then I was away from them, picking up speed. Samson seeming to understand that I needed to get away fast. I had the feeling that Samson and I had both just been released from some supernatural spell, and that now we were free. The flat field that connected the barn to the woods was only a soft blur below. Samson's galloping hoofs, and the red-gold of the setting sun seemed almost magical.

I wouldn't allow myself to feel any guilt for leaving Jonathan behind, for not waiting for him. I preferred to ride alone and that was that. Jonathan was nice, I had to admit, but he would just have to understand that I needed this time to myself. *By now,* I thought, *he's probably gotten the message.*

But as I neared the path to the woods, and as I slowed Samson down to a trot, I heard hoofbeats behind me. I knew it had to be Jonathan. He was following me.

Chapter 4

At the very beginning of the trail leading into Hagan's Woods, I brought Samson to a halt and turned in the saddle. I shouldn't have stopped, shouldn't have looked back. Jonathan had the kind of face you didn't look at — not if you were about to tell him to "Get lost." Just that one glance and *I* was the one who was lost. He was just too gorgeous.

"Hi," he said, catching up, letting Black Satin and Samson nuzzle each other. "You took off so fast. I didn't know . . ."

He hesitated, chewing his bottom lip. My habit, too. Suddenly I felt lots of sympathy for him. Now I knew for sure Jonathan wasn't always as self-assured as he appeared to be. That made me like him all the more.

It also made me kinder. I knew he was a little afraid of my reaction to his following me. "I don't mind riding together, only . . ."

"Only you hope I'm not going to disturb the

peace. I have a feeling riding and gabbing don't mix with you, am I right?"

I was pleased. "Right," I said. "I need to get away from it all sometimes. This is the only time."

He waved a hand and nodded. "Say no more. I won't say a word. I'll play by your rules. I won't say a word unless you do, okay? Silence will reign."

I had to smile. "Silence will reign," I repeated solemnly.

But even as I said it, words lined up in my mind, ready to slip past my lips. Suddenly there were hundreds of questions I wanted to ask him. After all, he had lived in Europe, he was a private-school boy, he had once lived in Springwood. But I pressed my lips together firmly and my knees against Samson's sturdy sides, and guided the horse along the narrow path. *Maybe later I'd talk to him,* I thought. *He'll spend lots of time at Hagan's, and maybe I . . .*

I forced myself to stop thinking about him. I was going much too fast. After all, I barely knew him, which made the funny feeling in my stomach and my slightly sweaty palms even more ridiculous. The stomach feelings, I realized, were the "butterflies" I had read about so much. Girls in books always got butterflies in their stomachs when they were near a boy they liked — or loved. Butterflies! It was a first. I had liked other boys; in fact, I'd had a few mad crushes. But no one had ever given me butterflies. I couldn't decide if I liked it or not.

Stop thinking about him. For a moment, I

wasn't sure if I had said that aloud. In my confusion, I gave Samson a small kick, and he speeded up. I didn't dare look behind me, although I could hear Black Satin following close behind.

Jonathan was true to his word. We rode for a long time, following the trails I chose, and he didn't speak once. At first, I was uncomfortable, self-conscious, but then I relaxed and began to enjoy having a silent companion. His presence didn't distract me. I could still notice all the small things that make me happy: a rabbit sitting upright on a stump, nose all pink and twitchy; the way the fading light turned the soft green ferns to a silvery blue-gray; the sweet mystery of the woods at twilight. I could still breathe in the moist, rich smells and listen to the sounds that pleased me. Jonathan wasn't any bother at all. In fact, I had to admit it, I liked Jonathan very much. I was glad I had met him. And I wanted to see more of him.

J. J. was in the barn when we got back, and either he was in a super-helpful mood, or he was playing Cupid. I guess he decided we needed more time together because he insisted on taking care of both Black Satin and Samson.

"Next time you can do it," J. J. said. "Tonight I just feel like keeping busy. Got too much energy today or something."

Jonathan didn't object and neither did I. But he didn't move or talk to me, and I couldn't think of a thing to say. We stood there, grinning foolishly at J. J. The silence was getting embarrassing, and

I wondered what had happened to all those questions I wanted to ask him.

I fiddled with the dangling sleeves of my sweater. Then, for something to do, I untied the knotted sleeves and pulled the sweater over my head. I wasn't cold, but I needed time to think. Under cover for a few seconds was just what I needed. When I emerged from my sweater I was ready.

"Well, I better be going," I said, cool as can be. "Nice meeting you, Jonathan. Will you be riding again soon?"

Suddenly he made his body all loose and floppy like a Raggedy Andy doll. "Whew!" he said, wiping his brow with one floppy hand. "Thank you!"

I stared at him. What was he thanking me for?

He winked at J. J. "I'm released from the spell." He said. "I can talk now — what a relief."

He came close and put one hand under my elbow. His voice was very soft. "Remember? I promised I wouldn't say a word until you did."

Now I was really embarrassed. I tried not to smile, but I didn't succeed. In fact, I laughed. "You are a *very* good boy," I said in my most motherly tone. "I'm proud of you."

He still had his hand under my elbow, and he led me from the barn out into the darkness that had suddenly replaced dusk.

"May I walk you home, Colleen? I'd like to, because I have lots of questions to ask you. Questions about Springwood — the way it is now. I bet I know some people that you know. Most of all, I want to know more about *you*."

In the darkness I could feel rather than see the intensity of his gaze, and his hand on my arm seemed to burn through my sweater. Talk about butterflies. My stomach was fluttering as if a thousand wings were in frantic motion.

I stood, almost hypnotized by his voice, his touch, the way his teeth reflected the only light which streamed from the barn window. I stood very still and wondered if it was possible to fall in love so fast. But even at that moment, which I wanted to last forever, a warning thought, like a red flag, came to spoil it. *Don't let him walk you home.*

If I let him walk me home, I would have to invite him in, introduce him properly to my family. I would have to present him for inspection — share him. My family wouldn't understand my not bringing him in to meet them. There was no such thing as a secret boyfriend in my house. Everyone, especially a great new friend, had to be welcomed, made to feel like "one of the family." Standard Kelly procedure. Nice, really, if you wanted your friends to feel like family. But I didn't want Jonathan to belong to anyone else but me. At least not yet.

"I really don't have time tonight," I said. "I have gobs of homework, and I was planning to jog home. Don't have time for conversation."

I sounded so cold and abrupt. I tried to soften it a little. "Maybe tomorrow, though. Will I see you here tomorrow?"

He didn't answer right away. "You're rather mysterious, do you know that?" he asked. "First, you don't let me talk, now you won't let me walk you home. Maybe you're not a real girl at all. Maybe you're someone I've dreamed up. Do you really exist, Colleen-with-the-amber-hair?"

All kinds of emotions raced through me. Laughter at his silliness, a strange ready-to-cry feeling, and excitement. How could one person, one boy, do this to me? A boy who was such a mixture of shyness and sureness and playfulness. He was still a stranger! How come at that moment I wanted to throw my arms around his neck, hold him tight, kiss him? I couldn't believe myself. I had to get away. *Right now*.

"See you tomorrow," I said over my shoulder as I ran toward the gate. I kept running, but I thought of one more thing to say.

"I am real, Jonathan," I shouted in his direction. Then under my breath, I whispered, "You'll see. You'll see how real I am."

Chapter 5

"*O*h, good, Colleen, you're home."

If I thought I was going to be able to come home unnoticed, find some little haven where I could flop, do my homework, and think about Jonathan, I was mistaken. The house was packed with people. Besides the usuals, there were guests — six more Kellys. The "Boston Kellys" had decided to drop in on the "New Jersey Kellys" on their way to Pennsylvania to visit the "Philadelphia Kellys." Here, unexpectedly, was Aunt Tessa (whom even my mother calls "gabby"), Uncle Francis ("fat and funny Franny," Nora calls him), and my cousins — all redheads, all boys, and all under twelve. Thank heavens they were not staying overnight.

"I wouldn't do that to you, Maggie," Aunt Tessa was telling Mom. "I mean, how ghastly!"

Suddenly her concerned face became a delighted one. "Colleen! Oh, Colleen, my love, come here to Aunt Tessa. Let me look at you."

I struggled to hold on to the image of Jonathan while Aunt Tessa held on to me. Aunt Tessa, like Mom, was the emotional type. She'd hug you like that even if she'd seen you only yesterday. I do love her, although she is a bit much sometimes!

As Aunt Tessa hugged and rocked, I wondered what would have happened if I had let Jonathan walk me home and invited him in. I shuddered inwardly. My own family is overwhelming enough. What would Jonathan think of *fourteen* red-headed Kellys, all talking and hugging, and acting like it was Christmas? He'd never make it, I decided.

Naturally, I had to stay downstairs and visit with them. If I didn't, Mom would never forgive me. Homework is not a legitimate excuse for escape. No matter how much my parents value education and respect studying, it comes second to guests. In our house people come first. Visitors mean food and drink and music and gossip and laughter and the bringing out of snapshots.

I knew what was coming the minute Uncle Francis commented on my riding boots.

"I thought I smelled stable," he said, grinning, after I told him I'd just returned from riding. "Nothing quite like the perfume of horseflesh."

As expected, Mom insisted I bring down my framed photograph of Samson. "You've never seen her brute, have you, Fran? Well, let me tell you he's positively frightening. How many hands high, Colleen? Anyway, love, go get the photo for Uncle Francis."

I heard her going on about Samson as I left the

living room. "Actually gentle as a lamb, you know. Shawn's gift to her on her fourteenth birthday."

In a way I was glad Mom sent me upstairs. It gave me a few moments of breathing space, a chance to try and recapture a clear picture of Jonathan, a sense of him to last until tomorrow. It was horrible how fast his face was fading from my mind, simply because I hadn't had enough time to let him develop permanently. You know? The way film develops?

I spent a few minutes sitting on the top step, my forehead pressed against the banister, trying to make sense of the feelings I'd had earlier. In books, love at first sight happens a lot, but in real life? Was it possible?

Just thinking the word "real" made me remember Jonathan's question again. "Are you real?" Was I so strange? Was I the only person in the world who liked and needed some peace and quiet?

I wanted so badly to just stay put and think about it some more, but I knew I had to return to the living room with Samson's photo. But getting the photo wasn't an easy thing at all. It meant wading through piles of magazines, sheets of poster board spread out on the carpeting, scissors and paste, magic markers. Not that I wasn't accustomed to having the bedroom transformed into a studio/workshop. Nora was always working on posters for whatever play she was appearing in, and her brand of creativity had never been neat. Maureen's current projects: her clothes, her hair, and the ever-present pile of writing and back of issues of *The Sun* made it even more difficult. I finally rescued Samson from under a pile of *Glamour* and *Mademoiselle*.

I sighed. Disorder made me almost as tired as noise did. And I resented having my few personal belongings moved around. More than ever I yearned for a room of my own.

Downstairs everyone was having a marvelous time: Even my three rambunctious cousins were content. They had discovered the Monopoly game which was kept in the piano bench, and now they were hot into the preliminaries, arguing about who would be banker, and who would handle the little green houses and red hotels. All very Kelly-ish. But Monopoly doesn't hold a candle to Kelly-style poker. You would never guess from the card-slapping and the yelling that they are only playing for plastic chips.

Anyway, Uncle Francis was making noises about "getting the show on the road," because, as he put it, "The Holiday Inn won't wait for us forever."

Aunt Tessa was ignoring him until he said, "I want to be on the road bright and early tomorrow."

Then she moaned and put her hands in her head. "And I thought this was supposed to be a vacation."

Despite my aunt's moans and groans and the noisy protests of the three boys, soon we were all clustered on the front porch saying good-bye to them. There was a big flurry of hugs and kisses and tears and fervent promises to "get together more often." I did my share of hugging and kissing but inwardly I was breathing a sigh of relief. At last I could be alone.

I was wrong. First there were dishes to collect, enough glasses and cups and plates to fill the dishwasher again. After I had rinsed the dishes, and wiped up the counter, I asked Mom if I could be excused.

"I hope you didn't have too much homework, Colleen." she said, twin furrows appearing between her eyebrows. "It's late."

"Not too much," I said, instantly thinking of Jonathan and my lie: "I have *gobs* . . ."

"Just two chapters for English," I said. "I'm going to read them in bed. We have a quiz tomorrow."

Mom's furrows got deeper. "Maybe it isn't such a good idea riding on school nights. At least, not on nights when you have homework."

"Samson has to have exercise," I said stiffly. "Every day. It's not fair to a horse not to let him run."

I was seething inside. Mom couldn't take that precious time at Hagan's away from me. Not now especially. I couldn't help thinking, *It's not Samson who's the problem, it's you. All of you.* But I didn't say that.

Instead I said very calmly and quietly, "Don't worry, Mom. I can handle the homework. I won't let riding interfere with it."

I kissed her good night and even managed a little smile. *What's the use?* I thought. Why even try to explain that in order to do my homework, to play junior hostess to friends and relatives, to endure the chaos of everyday life, I have to ride Samson? I was sure she wouldn't understand.

As I climbed the stairs, I heard two different kinds of music: Lynard Skynyrd from Rory and Patrick's room, and from our room, The Rolling Stones. The power switch to the tape players used in both rooms was second in importance only to the light switch. In the upstairs hall against the wall is one of Mom's treasures — a cuckoo clock. It was striking now.

Cuckoo. Cuckoo. Cuckoo. Ten damn times.

Added to that came the persistent drone of the TV, drifting upwards from the living room where my father was watching the ten o'clock news.

The minute I opened the door to our bedroom, Nora looked up from her cross-legged position on the carpet.

"Oh, great, Colleen, you're just in time. You've got a good eye. Tell me if my lettering's all right. Is it bright enough? I want these to be really eye-catching."

I took a deep breath. "Fine, Nora," I said. "It catches my eye just fine."

I didn't mention the fact that her name, as co-star, seemed much more eye-catching then even the name of the play. Not only did I not want to start a long discussion, but I figured Nora deserves it. She's a darned good actress, and since she does all the poster work, too, why shouldn't she put her own name in hot pink and the other words in pale blue?

"You've just got to meet Ronnie," she was saying now. "He is so adorable; I know you'll flip over him."

She smiled up at me, and said sweetly, "I'll answer all your questions about him. Anything you want to ask."

I didn't have any questions about her actor friend, not one. Certainly not now when I had Jonathan to wonder about.

"Can't right now, Nora," I said. "I have a quiz to study for. Have to read two whole chapters."

That didn't seem to faze her. She was still patting the carpet, smiling.

"An important test," I said. "First thing in the morning."

She seemed to get it then, but she looked disappointed. Nora needed an audience, and from the shower sounds and snatches of song coming from within our bathroom, her most loyal fan wasn't available. *Lucky Maureen,* I thought. All alone in the shower.

The image gave me a solution to my immediate problem. As soon as Maureen finished in the bathroom, I would escape there, lock the door, and find my solitude, no matter how brief, no matter how steamy.

When Maureen finally did emerge, wrapped from head to ankle in towels, she eyed me, my book, the clean pajamas in my hand, and shook her head from side to side.

"Unh unh," she said. "Sorry, but I think I just used up all the hot water. You'll have to wait at least a half hour."

She released the tangle of wet, dark red hair from the towel and began shaking her head like a dog. She didn't seem to notice that she was soaking Nora's posters until Nora shrieked.

"Stop that, Mo. See what you're doing? You're making my name run!"

Immediately Maureen was all apology, and I took that moment to seize the bathroom. Once inside, I locked the door and leaned against it. It was hard to breathe, even to see, the steam was so dense. But who cared? I would use the time until it cleared to get comfortable. When I was younger I used the bathtub as my quiet place. A thick bathmat beneath me, a rolled up towel as a pillow, and all cozy and happy, I would read my library book, or think-dream until inevitably I would be interrupted by urgent knocking and a "Hey, hurry up in there, will you?"

I undressed quickly, put on my pajamas, washed my face, and gave my hair and teeth a quick brushing. Then I made myself comfortable on the floor with the side of the tub as my backrest. I opened my book to Chapter Ten. I read the first paragraph six times before I gave up and gave in to Jonathan. I couldn't seem to stop thinking about him, so I decided why try. Actually it might be better if I got it all straight in my mind before tomorrow and I saw him again at Hagan's.

What if he didn't show up? What if I never saw him again? I realized I didn't really know a thing about him, even if he was going to live in Springwood now. Why hadn't I talked to him, let him talk to me?

"Colleen. *Colleen?*"

I closed my eyes so tight they hurt.

"Colleen, love? Let me in for just a minute, will you? You don't have to get out of the tub, just reach over and unlock the door for me. I don't know why you lock the door in the first place — we're sisters. Hurry up, I need the blower before my hair dries wrong. I want to read you something, too."

How would it feel to scream, I wondered. *One long bloodcurdling scream.* But I didn't. I closed my book, stood up, and opened the door.

Maureen stared at me in my pajamas then past me at the water running into the tub and uselessly down the drain.

"For heaven's sake, Colleen — what . . ."

I didn't stop. Just kept walking, stepping over the poster debris on the floor, opened the bedroom door, and closed it behind me.

Then I did stop. Now what? Where could I go now? Grandpa Shawn had gone up to his room on the third floor right after the Boston Kellys left. He was probably still up reading or perhaps writing.

I walked quickly to the door of the stairway leading up to his room and knocked. *I should have done this first,* I told myself. *Grandpa Shawn won't let me down.*

Chapter 6

When I knocked and there was no answer, I figured he had closed the door at the top of the stairs, too. Unusual but possible. Maybe he was trying to shut out the downstairs noise, too. But when I climbed to the top of the narrow, carpeted stairway, his door was open, and I could see him sitting stone still on the edge of his bed in his pajamas. It surprised me; Grandpa Shawn is a night owl. As he says, he's always "burning the midnight oil." I didn't expect him to be ready for bed.

It was obvious he hadn't heard me coming up the stairs, and I didn't want to startle him out of what seemed to be really deep thought, so I rapped lightly on the door frame and spoke softly.

"Hi," I said. "It's me. I was hoping to hide out with you for a while, but I see you're ready for bed so . . ."

The way he raised his silvery head, the way it took so long for his eyes to focus on my face, that long, long moment before I was sure he actually saw me, scared me, made my heart start beating very fast. Something was wrong.

I hurried to his side and knelt in front of him, searching his face for reassurance. There was something strange about his face and it took a few seconds until I realized what it was. He looked old. Grandpa Shawn looked wrinkled and tired and frail. I was shocked. Sure, he's seventy-three, but honestly, he has never looked old to me. Mature, dignified, but never old.

All this was going on inside; outwardly I spoke to Grandpa Shawn, putting my hand over his hand and squeezing.

"Are you all right?" I asked urgently. "Do you feel all right? Is there anything I can do for you?"

Then, like a miracle, he changed back into the Grandpa Shawn I knew. Almost. At least, his eyes seemed to come to blue life, and his voice sounded normal.

"I'm fine, Collie," he said, "except maybe for a wee touch of the blahs! Or maybe, as they say, some acid indigestion. My own fault, of course. I should have known better."

He pointed to his mouth and then his chest. "Onions," he explained. "Onions and I are not good friends. We are not compatible."

"How about some Alka-Seltzer?" I said, relieved. For a few minutes he'd had me worried. "Or I could fix you a bicarb cocktail? That should take care of the enemy."

He smiled at me and then leaned over and kissed the top of my head.

"That would be lovely, darlin' — some bicarb might just do the trick. Now, why didn't I think of that myself?"

I got up and hurried to his bathroom where I knew he kept baking soda and a glass. *I'll have him feeling fine in a jiffy,* I thought, feeling suddenly very efficient and superior. He was so foolish to eat something he knew would disagree with him. Dad does that, too. Hot peppers and sour pickles and liverwurst and onions. They were gluttons for punishment, both of them.

But he didn't laugh at the little lecture I gave him, and he didn't drink the cloudy mixture I handed him, nor did he act as if he wanted me to stay. I was puzzled and a little hurt, too, when he said, "I think I'll turn in now, Colleen. I'm really quite tired tonight. Maybe we can postpone your visit until tomorrow, if you don't mind."

He wasn't looking at me — his head was bent slightly — and I got the impression that it was hard for him to talk.

But I pushed away my hurt and the little knot of fear in my stomach. He was so uncomfortable.

" 'Course I don't mind," I said. "I just hope you feel better in the morning."

He was still holding the glass.

"Drink it all up now," I said, and in a teasing voice I added, "Like a good boy."

His smile was slow but sweet. "Ah, and you're a good girl, Collie. Thank you."

I kissed him on the cheek and left him sitting there. I went down the stairs and straight to my room, trying not to feel too disappointed. Maybe by now Maureen and Nora were winding down. I would read my chapters first thing in the morning. I already knew the material quite well anyway. I would use the time before sleep to think-dream.

Think-dream about Jonathan Holmes, naturally. Who else?

Hurrying feet in the hall. Someone running down the stairs. A door opening, closing. A strange high-pitched hum — voices. Class would begin any minute.

In my dream I was at my desk reading, alone in an empty classroom, first-period English. Soon we would be taking the quiz and I was nervous because I really wasn't that well prepared. The teacher and the other kids were late. In my mind, or from somewhere, I heard the words: "Too late."

I couldn't shake the feeling of dread. *Too late?* What had happened? Had something terrible happened to the teacher and all the students? Maybe I better go and see.

I stared down at my open book and the words disappeared, leaving only blank pages, emptiness. The desk disappeared and then the chair. I was suspended in air and frightened. The dread got stronger and I *knew* — something terrible had happened.

The dream began all over again. First the sound of running feet, a door closing, a high-pitched voice.

Our door opened, and I blinked frantically in

the sudden glare of the overhead light. It was Mom's voice, tense, full of alarm.

"*Maureen. Nora. Colleen.* Hurry, get up. I need you. Grandpa Shawn is . . ."

I didn't wait for her to finish the sentence. I didn't want her to finish the sentence. I was out of bed and running into the hall, up the steps to the third floor. Wide, wide awake, a surge of something powerful flooding every part of my body. I seemed to fly up the stairs, my feet not even touching the steps. *I had to hurry.*

Grandpa Shawn's bed was empty. The room was empty. I saw the still full glass of bicarb and water on the table beside his bed, and his brown leather slippers on the floor. Otherwise, his room was neat, quiet, softly lit.

Where was he? What had happened to Grandpa Shawn?

Mom had said — *what*?

I raced down the stairs, nearly colliding with Patrick and Nora, who stood groggy and bewildered in the upstairs hall.

"What's the matter?" I said, my voice too loud in the silence.

But I didn't wait for an answer. I could scarcely breathe. I ran down the second flight of stairs.

Then for a long moment I stopped breathing altogether. Grandpa Shawn was on the couch, his eyes closed, the color of his face nearly matching his hair and mustache. He wasn't moving. I let out a long breath and drew in another one, as if by doing that I could help him breathe. *Was* he breathing?

Then I heard his voice. A weak voice, but his voice. Grandpa Shawn was alive.

"I guess it wasn't the onions, darlin'," he said, not opening his eyes.

He knew I was there. Without opening his eyes, my grandfather knew I was there beside him. I felt weak with tenderness as well as dread.

I could hear Dad on the phone in the hall. "Yes. Yes — we've called them. The ambulance should be here any minute. Fine, Dr. Prine. Yes, we'll see you at the hospital."

Mom came in to the living room with a bed pillow and motioned to me to lift Grandpa Shawn's head.

"Maybe this will make you more comfortable, Shawn," she said, "until the First Aiders arrive."

Mom's face, usually so bright, was very pale. "Grandpa Shawn's having some trouble with his heart. It's best if we get him some good care as soon as possible."

I was a little surprised at her self-control, but then I remembered. Mom gets all emotional and shook up about little things, but in a crunch, when anything big or bad happens, she's always a rock. I knew I could depend on her to tell me the truth.

I stared at her hard. She got the message. She nodded her head up and down, and I relaxed a little. Mom was telling me he had a good chance, that I should be calm and not panic.

I thought I had better follow her example. The last thing Grandpa Shawn needed was hysterical people around him. I knelt beside him and put my hand lightly on his shoulder. I just wanted him to know I was there, that I would always be there when he needed me. I didn't expect him to talk.

But he did. "Don't worry, Collie. They'll probably fix me up better than ever."

He stopped talking abruptly and I felt his body tense beneath my hand, and saw his face tighten up. He was in pain.

But it seemed to pass, and he finished what he wanted to say. ". . . and I'll be home soon. I'm taking a rain check on our little visit."

Then the Springwood First Aiders were in the room, rolling with them a narrow, wheeled cot. The men worked surely and swiftly, and before I knew it Grandpa Shawn was in the ambulance and Dad was climbing in behind him.

The rest of us stood watching the ambulance pull away from the curb until the flashing lights disappeared around the corner. It was still very dark. It had turned very cold, too. Rory was the first one to speak, saying, "It's almost four o'clock."

Knowing the time made it easier somehow. It made everything solid and real again. Not that I wasn't still scared and worried, but it wasn't a nameless dread anymore; at least the dread had a name.

The name was "heart attack." Mom told us all about it on the way to the hospital.

"He was just sitting there on the bed, and I know it took all his strength to call out loud enough for us to hear him. He said he knew he was having an attack; that's why he didn't try to make it down the stairs. Patrick, your father, and Rory carried him down to the living room."

She hesitated only a bit. "Your grandfather is in excellent shape for a man his age. He's always taken very good care of himself. I know that will be in his favor."

I knew she was trying to reassure us and maybe herself, too. Why hadn't I realized that he was really sick and in pain? I shouldn't have been thinking about myself so much. Grandpa Shawn and I both should have known better.

Dread and guilt were heavy on my chest. And I was still having trouble with my breathing. I felt horrible and uneasy, and frightened.

If anything happened to Grandpa Shawn . . .

Chapter 7

Grandpa Shawn was already in the Intensive Care Unit at Galen General Hospital. He wasn't allowed visitors yet, but in the words of the crisply pretty nurse at the desk, he was "doing as well as can be expected." The heart attack had been "relatively mild," she told us, and chances were good for a complete recovery.

Some of the awful heaviness in my chest went away.

Dr. Prine appeared in the doorway and I sat up straighter. I tried to read his face — good news or bad?

But he didn't add much to what we already knew.

"I think we can be cautiously optimistic," Dr. Prine said. The next twenty-four hours is the most dangerous period, and for ten days after that we will monitor him carefully and hope he doesn't have another episode."

My mother, the rock-in-a-crisis, was beginning to crumble now that the worst was over.

I felt shaky, too. And tired. My eyelids felt gritty and the coffee from the machine was making me feel sick.

Looking around, I could see that everyone was fading fast. Nora had bluish smudges under her eyes, and Patrick sat with his shoulders slumped. For a change, no one had much to say. Then Rory took a deep breath and began organizing.

"Dad, Mom — you two go home now. Catch a nap and shower. I'll stay here with Grandpa Shawn. No sense in us all hanging around."

That sparked a family conference, and it was decided that we would all take turns, that at every moment, night and day, one member of the family would be at the hospital standing watch. Rory would keep the vigil first, then Patrick. Dad, Mom, Nora, and Maureen would go to work, and I would stay home from school to answer the phone.

Leaving the hospital, I was stunned by the brilliance of the morning. Somehow I expected it to be still the middle of the night, dark and eerily quiet. The leaves on the trees dotting the hospital grounds caught the early-morning sun and made the morning all gold and orange-bright. I didn't want to acknowledge the beauty of it. *The day has no right to be so nice,* I thought. Not with Grandpa Shawn lying up there so helpless and alone.

When we got home, Mom insisted we all have breakfast as usual. Everyone seemed to think that was a great idea, and soon the kitchen buzzed with activity and the air was fragrant with the smell of frying bacon and toast. Maybe everyone was really hungry, maybe not. Personally I think just the ordinariness of breakfast helped, made the world seem back to normal.

But soon they all went their own ways, leaving me alone. The house became loud with noises I had never noticed before. The refrigerator hummed, the floor in the front hall creaked beneath my feet, and the kitchen sink faucet dripped a steady "tink-tink" no matter how tight I turned it.

For a while I wandered around downstairs, and then settled down on the couch where Grandpa Shawn had lain only a few hours before. Lying there comforted me, made me feel closer to him. It felt good to sink into the deep cushions, to let my body relax for the first time. I wouldn't sleep, of course, but it wouldn't hurt to just close my eyes for a minute. . . .

The phone was ringing!

I came awake suddenly, sharply. The phone. I hadn't meant to fall asleep. Dazed, feeling guilty, I ran to the kitchen and grabbed up the receiver just as the phone rang again. How loud it sounded in the silent room.

"Hello?" I said, forcing steadiness into my voice. "Hello?"

"May I speak to Colleen, please?"

I plopped straight down into a sitting position on the floor, my legs rubbery with relief.

The phone call didn't have anything to do with

Grandpa Shawn. It had to do with me. It was Jonathan.

"Oh, hi, Jonathan," I said. "How are you?"

He sounded happy.

"Good. You didn't forget my name at least."

I thought *no way,* but I didn't say that. Suddenly I realized that during all the early morning hours, even later while I was alone in the house, I hadn't thought of him once. Now, hearing his voice, his face appeared in my mind — the gray eyes, the deep tan, the smile.

"Cloverdale Road isn't very far from where I live," he was saying. "If you're going riding today, I could drive over and pick you up."

"Jonathan, how do you know I live on Cloverdale Road?"

He laughed. "I went over to the high school a little while ago. Thought I might see you when school let out. I was hanging around, and finally I got up my nerve and asked someone. I happened to choose your best friend. She said you weren't in school, but she told me where you lived and gave me your phone number."

My best friend?

"Is she short with curly dark hair? Huge dark eyes?"

"That's the one," he said. "Friendly."

Shari Brubaker. Oh, Lord. That meant the third degree when I went back to school...

"Anyway, Colleen, how about it? May I pick you up? You tell me when and I'll be there."

His voice was so deep and clear. His eagerness

to see me brought back the butterflies. I touched my cheeks with my free hand. They were very warm, and I knew if I looked in the mirror at that moment, they would be fever-bright. How could one boy have such a powerful effect on me? Then I remembered.

"Oh, Jonathan, I can't. Not today, anyway."

There was a long pause while I thought about what to say. He broke the silence first. "Colleen, is anything wrong?"

"Well, yes. You see, my grandfather is in the hospital. He had a heart attack last night. I have to stay at home and answer the phone. And we're taking turns at the hospital. It's kind of . . . a hard time."

I realized as I was talking that I had said more just now than I had during more than an hour yesterday. "In fact, I shouldn't be tying up the phone now. My brother might be trying to call . . . you know, from the hospital." I hadn't meant my voice to break, but it did.

"Hey, Colleen — I'm really sorry. Is there anything I can do? Would you like some company? Someone to wait with? I could come over now and . . ."

"No, no," I said quickly, and his silence made me aware of how ungrateful I sounded.

"I mean, thanks, Jonathan, but everything's kind of confusing around here. No one has had any sleep and I guess you better not . . ."

He cut off my apologies. "I understand," he said quietly. "I hope everything will be all right.

And if I can help, please let me know. Before you hang up, write down my number. If you need a ride to visit your grandfather, or anything . . ."

"Thanks," I said, memorizing the number he gave me. "You're very nice, Jonathan."

I was close to tears again, and I wasn't quite sure why. Maybe it was just the deep, quiet voice that sounded so caring. Maybe it was just the simple fact that I was so tired.

"Colleen," he said. "When everything is okay, we'll go riding." Now his voice was very soft. "I hope . . . soon."

"Me, too," I whispered. " 'Bye, Jonathan."

I sat there on the hard tile floor for the longest time, the receiver still clutched in my hand. I kept my finger pressed on the disconnect button, though; I couldn't let the phone stay busy. Finally I stood up and placed the receiver back on the hook.

It would have been nice to say, "Yes, Jonathan, come over. Sit with me. Be my friend today." But I didn't want him here, not yet. Now, with everything so uncertain, it wasn't a very good time to introduce him to the family.

I felt a tiny stab of something unpleasant. It took me a few seconds to realize it was guilt. The reason I didn't want Jonathan here was the same reason as I'd had yesterday. I didn't want to share him. I didn't want my feelings for him spread out on the dining room table. Jonathan was private.

Anyway, I reasoned, Jonathan seemed like the quiet, thoughtful type. He probably wouldn't understand my family or fit in very well. I had a feeling he needed calmness and quiet just as much as I did. *That's why I'm so attracted to him,* I decided. Because he is so much like me. In that case, I was doing him a favor. As soon as possible I would call him and tell him to meet me at Hagan's.

Chapter 8

"*Y*ou sneak!" Shari said on Monday when I went back to school. "Why didn't you tell me? Where on earth did you find him?"

Shari had to tell me in detail about the afternoon Jonathan had come to Springwood High looking for me.

"I'm glad I happened to be handy," she said. "Wasn't that lucky? Did he call you? Or come over?"

I had to admit Jonathan had chosen wisely. Shari Brubaker is an information booth. She knows everyone, everything. I don't mean to say I don't like Shari. I do. What I like about her most is her enthusiasm. Of course, what I like least is her nosiness. Still, even that is because she really is interested in people; even her gossip is never intentionally mean. I decided I would have to tell her about Jonathan. A little bit, anyway. Which is all I could tell her. I didn't know very much myself.

"His name is Jonathan Holmes and I only met him once — at Hagan's. He lived in Springwood when he was little. He has a beautiful horse," I added lamely.

"Yes," Shari said impatiently. "But are you going out with him? He must like you a lot if he came looking for you. Colleen, you *have* to like him, too — he's absolutely gorgeous. How old is he?"

"He's eighteen," I told her.

Now Shari narrowed her eyes and smiled slyly. "Want to know how he described you?"

How? Sure, I wanted to know — naturally. But I just shrugged. "Shari, honestly. I barely know him."

She told me anyway. I was glad my show of nonchalance hadn't stopped her.

"He said: 'Do you know a girl named Colleen? She has amber-colored hair and eyes like smoke.' I thought it was so neat for him to say that. Colleen, I have to admit I couldn't think what color amber was. I guess he noticed 'cause he said, 'You know, a pale copper like an old penny.'

"Gads, Colleen, he's so romantic the way he talks. Anyway, so I said then, 'Of course I know her. Colleen is my closest friend.' I told him you weren't in school and then I gave him your phone number and told him where you lived. Colleen, I hope that was the right thing to do. I just figured you wouldn't want him to get away."

Shari gave herself a little hug and smiled dreamily. "I know I sure wouldn't."

I was glad when the bell rang and we had to go

our separate ways. I wasn't ready to tell her how I already felt about him. I wasn't ready to tell anyone! If I thought of Shari as nosy, she was mild compared to Maureen and Nora. Multiply by fifty. Maureen, for instance, is fond of saying that she can get people to say things they really didn't mean to say. Which makes her a good reporter but a dangerous person to live with.

Monday was a good day, though. I felt wonderful. Grandpa Shawn was doing fine. Sometime during the day, he was going to be transferred out of Intensive Care and moved to a regular room.

After school I was heading straight for Galen General for my first visit. I couldn't wait to see him. Home hadn't seemed right without him. Mom and Dad were at the hospital a lot, and Dad was allowed to see him for a few minutes at a time.

"I know he's feeling better," Dad said, laughing. "He's complaining about the food."

I had something else exciting to think about. After I came home from seeing Grandpa Shawn, after dinner, I was going to call Jonathan. I was going to tell him I was going to Hagan's and ask him if he wanted to ride with me. I thought I should call him. After all, he had called me.

But, as it turned out, after supper I got nervous and changed my mind. I just couldn't call him. I stood there with my hand on the phone for the longest time, but I couldn't make myself dial the number I had memorized. I just couldn't.

I did spend extra time on my face and hair,

though, and I changed into my best-fitting jeans and a new heathery gold sweater that almost matched my hair. I even put my best gold chain around my neck. Just in case. Just in case Jonathan showed up on his own.

He did! He was already there when I arrived, and his wide smile and the eager "hi" he gave me told me that he had been hoping I would show up.

It was a repeat of the first time. He followed behind me on Black Satin and when I turned, he pressed a finger to his lips and nodded slowly, telling me wordlessly that he was going to follow the rule I had set: No talking!

This time I took the trail that leads to Squirrel Brook, where more than once I have seen deer and where a family of beavers have their headquarters. I wanted to share this favorite spot with Jonathan because I knew he would like it as much as I did. We stayed on our horses and watched the beavers swim from one side of the brook to another like small, jet-propelled submarines, leaving behind them streaks of silver water. I was having trouble with the butterflies again. Every time I looked at him, each time our eyes met, I felt something happen to my stomach, and my heart didn't seem to be beating as it should.

We were heading back across the field, Samson and Black Satin side by side, when he reached out and touched my shoulder signaling me to stop. He pointed to his mouth and lifted his tilty eyebrows.

"Yes," I said, laughing a little. "Speak."

"How's your grandfather, Colleen? And will you meet me here tomorrow night?"

"He's better," I said, and the next words tumbled out fast, "Yes, I will; I'll meet you here tomorrow."

There was no question in my mind about that.

"That's good," he said softly.

Black Satin and Samson had moved close to each other, nuzzling and making friendly sounds. It meant that Jonathan and I were very close, too. Close enough to touch.

Then I felt his hand on my hair. He lifted a curl and held it away from my neck, and then replaced it gently. The tips of his fingers brushed my cheek gently.

"I've been thinking about you, Colleen. So much. I wondered . . ."

I turned to look at him. His eyes had turned dark as slate.

"Wondered what, Jonathan?"

He was leaning toward me now. "If you were someone I dreamed up. You're so . . . I think you're beautiful, Colleen."

I have never felt beautiful in my life. Nice-looking sometimes, never beautiful. Now I did, and it gave me a strange, powerful feeling. Jonathan thought I was beautiful.

"I'm real," I said, looking him straight in the eye. "I'm quite real."

His mouth seemed to soften, and the corners turned up slightly. I couldn't stop looking at his mouth.

"I'm glad," he whispered. "I'm so glad."

Then his mouth was covering mine, for a moment that seemed endless and too brief at the same time. I wanted to drop Samson's reins and put both arms around Jonathan's neck and let him know how much I liked his kiss. I wanted him to kiss me again. But I didn't. Instead, I pulled away.

"Jonathan . . ." I said, not knowing what to say.

Maybe he thought I was annoyed. Maybe he thought I wasn't happy about him kissing me because he said, "Too fast for you, Colleen? Don't worry, I'll go slower. It's just that I've never felt this way about a girl before. Believe that, Colleen. It's true."

We began to ride again and I was glad the light was fading. Even though I hadn't told him how I felt, or that I hadn't minded him kissing me at all, I knew I really did need more time.

This time we didn't let J. J. take care of Samson and Black Satin. Looking after the horses and putting them back in their stalls gave us some easy time together. Now we did talk but not about us. Mostly about other people: the Hagans, and Mrs. Duncan the librarian, whom Jonathan remembered well.

"She liked me, I guess, because I was, as she put it, 'such a quiet little boy, so well-behaved.' Plus, she liked it that I could read well."

I liked that, too. Immediately, we were talking about books, comparing favorite authors, telling each other what books we were reading at the moment. He recommended some to me and I recommended some to him. Finally, just before I said good-bye to him I asked him the most important question. The one I *had* to ask him.

"Are you staying here, Jonathan? I mean, are you going to live in Springwood now?"

I held my breath. Don't let him say he's just visiting. Don't let him fly off to London or Switzerland or *anywhere*, I prayed silently.

"Oh, sure," he said, his eyebrows lifting in surprise. "Didn't I tell you that?" He frowned. "No, come to think of it, I guess I didn't. His frown became a faint smile. "Haven't had much chance to tell you anything."

"That's right," I said, not smiling. "Silence has been reigning a lot."

"Like cats and dogs," he said, nodding solemnly. "Anyway, yes, we'll be living here again. My parents have taken over my grandmother's house on the lake. Grandma died this past spring. Dad grew up here, and Mom always liked the old house. It needs a lot of work, but that's my mother's hobby anyway — antiques. I'll be going to Rutgers in January. Right now I'm just taking some courses I need at Middlesex."

But I wasn't listening very hard. All I kept thinking was that he wasn't going to fly away, disappear out of my life.

"Good," I said. "I'll see you tomorrow. Same time."

I left him standing there, and I ran toward the gate without looking back. As I ran I kept thinking, *Same time tomorrow.* I thought of something else too: Maybe he'll kiss me again, *same time tomorrow.*

I was in love with Jonathan Holmes. And I thought he was in love with me, too. And Grandpa Shawn would get well.

Everything was wonderful.

Chapter 9

The next evening, and for the next four evenings, we met and rode and talked, and on the third night he kissed me again.

"I'm trying not to rush you," he said. "I don't want to scare you away."

"Don't worry," I said, and lifted my lips for another kiss.

That made him laugh. "Maybe *I* should be scared," he said.

By now we were comfortable with each other, and our meetings took on a definite pattern and rhythm that I liked very much.

We would gallop across the field to the edge of the woods, canter where the trail is wide and clear of overhanging branches, then slow down to a trot. Finally, at the point where the brush is thickest, and the trail narrowest, we would let Samson and Black Satin walk, let them decide how best to go. We didn't use words and we didn't need words.

On Friday night, Jonathan admitted that he preferred to ride in silence, too.

"I guess it's because I've done all my riding by myself. Talking is fine, but if you talk when you're on a horse I think you forget to notice things."

I must have smiled when he told me that because he said, "I can see you approve of that."

"Yes, I do," I said seriously. "I don't know of any other person who thinks like that. Who understands. Most of the kids I know like to make everything a party."

Jonathan nodded. "I think it's because most people are afraid of silences. They get nervous."

I almost told him about my noisy family, but I stopped just in time. I wasn't ready to share him, nor was I ready to share them.

He asked me to meet him the next day. "Tomorrow is Saturday," he said. "Something new for us, riding in sunlight and for more than an hour at a time. Can you?"

I hesitated. If all went well, we could bring Grandpa Shawn home tomorrow. Rory and Dad and I were driving to the hospital around noon. I couldn't just run off on the day of Grandpa Shawn's homecoming. It was very possible I'd be needed to sit with him, be his nurse at least part of the day. I hoped Jonathan would understand.

He did. "Tell you what," he said. "I'll call you around three. By that time you should know if you'll be able to get away for a while. If you can, then I'll scoot over and pick you up."

"Tell *you* what," I said quickly. "I'll call *you*

when I know for sure, okay? I know your phone number by heart. Aren't you flattered?"

I teased him so he wouldn't notice how I'd evaded his phone call. Jonathan noticed.

"I think I would be more flattered if you'd let me pick you up or phone." His eyes were dark gray clouds. I had hurt his feelings.

"Oh, Jonathan," I said. "It's just that things are so hectic at our house — my grandfather being sick and all. It's easier for me to call you, meet you. Really, that's all it is."

"Sure, Colleen. I can understand that. My parents for instance . . ."

He stopped in mid-sentence. "Hey, who wants to talk about parents? There still so much I don't know about you. Colleen, promise if we get a few hours together tomorrow, we'll bend the rules a little. I have so many questions to ask you."

"Me, too," I said eagerly. It was the truth. In the past week, even with the usual distractions at home and school, I had thought of a long list of questions. After only ten days I knew enough to love him. Anything I learned about him wouldn't change that.

Grandpa Shawn was very quiet on the way home from the hospital. Ten days in Galen General had taken ten pounds and the color from his skin. He looked smaller, paler, very tired. I kept glancing at him out of the corner of my eye. I guess he was aware of my doing that, because when Dad pulled the car into the driveway,

Grandpa reached over and squeezed my hand reassuringly.

"Now I'll be fine," he said. "I kept from going berserk by thinking of all this."

He made a sweeping motion with one hand to indicate the house, the yard, the bright noon sun shining on the golden chrysanthemums.

Then he pointed upward toward the third floor windows. "Especially there," he said, sighing happily. "My haven."

I knew what he meant. The night before, I had escaped to his room. I knew he wouldn't mind, and I really needed time alone to review the time with Jonathan. I sat for over two hours cuddled up in the blue wing chair, and by the time I went downstairs to join the family, I was sure that I had Jonathan's face and voice firmly in my mind. I knew I would be able to produce his picture, his sound whenever I wanted to now.

After Grandpa Shawn was settled in his room and lunch was over, Mom asked for a volunteer to stay home and "keep an eye out."

I smiled at that. When we were still little enough to need a baby-sitter but big enough to feel insulted, she used to say that.

"I know you children don't really need supervision. I know you're very *good* children. I just like to have someone here so you can go to sleep, someone to keep an eye out."

Anyway, I knew Mom was sparing Grandpa Shawn, allowing for the dignity of his age. Wouldn't he despise needing a baby-sitter?

Every month Mom chairs the meeting of the Friends of the Library. This meeting was very special. Mary Lund Wheeler, the best-selling mystery writer, was the guest speaker; Mom adores her books. It would kill her if she missed hearing her talk.

"I'll stay if necessary," she said.

No one would hear of it.

Nora sighed. "I'd stay, too, but today is dress rehearsal."

She paused. "Well, actually, it's *pre*-dress rehearsal. But we open Friday."

Mom patted Nora's hand. "You go, love. I know how hard you've been working."

"Oh, heavens," Maureen said. "I have an interview with the new pastor at St. Michael's — *in ten minutes!*"

She was up and away, running a comb through her hair as she ran.

Patrick, I knew, had film to develop. He couldn't keep a proper eye out in his basement darkroom.

Dad and Rory had already left the house. Saturday afternoons were their time at *The Sun*: story-writing, editing, clearing their desks of unfinished business.

I tried not to mind. What was so terrible? When had I ever minded being alone with Grandpa Shawn. Since when? Since Jonathan. I would have to call him.

I dialed his number after everyone went their separate ways.

"Hi, Jonathan," I said. "Bad news. I won't be

able to meet you today. I have to . . . I want to spend some time with my grandfather."

Even as I said the words I was thinking: *He answered the phone on the first ring.* He must have been sitting by the phone, waiting for my call. It gave me a funny feeling inside.

He sighed. "I figured," he said. "I know how worried you've been. I guess you and your grandfather are very close."

"Yes, we are," I said, "But it's not just that. Everyone else has appointments, or work today. I *have* to stay."

I could hear the relief in his voice. "I understand, Colleen. Your grandfather comes first. Anyway, I thought this might happen, so I have another plan. Plan B, I call it."

"What?" I asked. "What's Plan B?"

"Plan B is tomorrow," he said. "Plan B calls for riding at one P.M. tomorrow afternoon. Sunday dinner at my house afterward. My mother said she would call and invite you."

"Oh, that's okay," I said hastily. "She doesn't have to. Just tell her it's all right. Tell her I'd be happy to come."

Mrs. Holmes couldn't call. What if she started talking to Mom?

"Great," Jonathan said. "Want me to pick you up at one?"

"I'll meet you at Hagan's," I said firmly. "At one. Is it okay if I come to dinner in riding clothes?"

Jonathan's long hesitation confused me. Did his parents have an objection to "the perfume of horseflesh"?

"Sure," he said. "To tell the truth, I hadn't thought of that."

Then he laughed. "Don't worry about it. Who cares what you wear? Not me. Anyway, I'll see you at one, Colleen."

All afternoon I kept thinking about it. Did it matter how I dressed? Why would it? In our house, except for very special occasions, any outfit is acceptable so long as we are clean and brushed and decently covered. Why had I said yes? It really wasn't a very good idea to accept an invitation to Jonathan's house. Because it meant very soon, I would have to do the same. I would have to invite him for Sunday dinner at my house, introduce him to *my* family. I wasn't ready for that. No way!

Chapter 10

*S*hari is right; I can be sneaky. Sunday morning, for instance.

I knew I had to tell Mom I wouldn't be home for dinner that day. Sunday dinner is special at our house, the day for guests and best china, and Mom always tries to do some kind of pretty centerpiece for the table, usually cut flowers from Dad's garden. Sunday is also the day when Dad does the cooking. He's a great cook but wants us all there to eat the results.

I waited until almost eleven when Mom was rushing around searching for her notebook, her favorite pen, and the green Liberty scarf she likes to wear with her white wool blazer. I waited until she was at the peak of her frenzy, the instant she decided her car keys would *never* be found.

"Why does this always happen to me?" she wailed as usual.

Mom is always misplacing her car keys.

She had an appointment at the Sheraton Motor

Hotel with Mary Lund Wheeler. Mom was very excited about it.

Now as I helped in the search for the missing car keys, I said, ever so casually, "A friend I ride with at Hagan's invited me over for dinner today. I'm afraid I accepted already. I hope it's all right with you."

Before she could answer, I handed her the missing keys which I'd found several minutes earlier.

"Oh, thank heavens," she said, moving quickly toward the front door. "I'll see you later, love. Have a good time."

It took me quite a while to decide what to wear. Finally I chose the gray wool pants I had bought last year. They fit me like a dream. I decided to wear my riding boots and my rust pullover, but I would bring my good black boots in a bag and my best lemon-yellow cashmere. After riding and before Jonathan brought me to his house I would change the sweater and boots in a dark corner of the barn. At the last minute I added a pretty paisley scarf and the gold stud earrings Nora had given me last Christmas. When I left the house I was satisfied, but as I neared Hagan's, I wasn't so sure. Maybe I should wear a skirt to dinner instead of pants? Would his parents disapprove? Would Jonathan? I wanted to look my best.

I needn't have worried. The look in his eyes told me how he felt.

He looked super-handsome. He was wearing camel-colored corduroys, a shirt to match, with a tweedy jacket with leather patches on the elbows. Young country gentleman — *that* look.

I caught J. J. staring at Jonathan.

"What's the matter, J. J.?" I asked.

"Oh, nothing," he said, then blurted, "You guys going riding dressed like *that?*"

Jonathan laughed. "You forget, I'm a man of the world. I've traveled abroad. You heard your mother. And Colleen here . . . well, she is just naturally elegant."

He couldn't have chosen a better word. I had a hunch that Jonathan's parents would appreciate "elegance" more than any other quality. Just a hunch, probably based on the fact that Jonathan always looked like that. My first impression — an aristocrat. His parents, I was sure, would be like that, too.

Black Satin and Samson seemed very happy to be close to each other. We laughed about it and decided we were on a "double date."

"I think they have something going, don't you?" Jonathan asked me.

"Why not?" I answered him breezily.

He looked at me seriously. "You're right, Colleen. Why not?"

I knew he wasn't talking about our horses' budding romance.

This time, as we rode, we talked a lot. I learned more about him than in all the other times put together, and nothing he said disappointed me. Not only was he handsome and sensitive and soft-spoken, he was interesting. He told me his plans for the future.

"When I was small, when I lived here, Grandmother Holmes let me help her in the garden. She gave me my own space, a few directions, a handful of seeds, and left me alone. That's when I discovered I had a green thumb."

He held up a thumb and wiggled it under my nose. "See my green thumb?"

I laughed. "Gee, I never noticed that before, Jonathan. It really is very, very green."

He grinned. "You would have noticed sooner if you'd held my hand more often."

We were at a wide point in the trail; Black Satin and Samson were walking side by side. Jonathan reached over and took my hand in his. For as long as possible we rode like that and Jonathan told me more.

"I really like seeing things grow, and more than that, I like planning the spaces in any given area. I drive around sometimes and look at houses, office buildings, factories, places like that, and imagine what I could do with them. Trees, shrubs, flowers, the right arrangement. Colleen, it would be so simple to make even very ugly places beautiful."

He hesitated for a moment. "I don't know why it took me so long to realize I had to be a landscape architect. I wasted so much time taking courses I wasn't interested in. My father just assumed I would go into law. I just drifted along with that until last spring. I saw some gardens at a home outside of London and I knew."

He paused and looked at me. "That seems to be happening a lot."

"Yes," I said simply. It had happened to me, too.

Something else. Every minute I spent with him, I fell more in love with him. If tenderness, and wonder, and a feeling of being exactly where I should be, of doing exactly what I wanted to do, of being with the right person, is love, I was sure it was — especially at that moment.

He had tightened his hand around mine. "Never lose that look in your eyes, Colleen," he said very quietly.

He knew. I just smiled.

But on the way to his house an hour later, I didn't feel quite so good. I was nervous! I had never had a boy invite me home for dinner to meet his parents. Most likely because boys in Springwood didn't do that. They would come to your house any time you asked, but not the other way around. Plus the fact that I had never been serious about anyone before, and to the best of my knowledge, no one had felt that strongly about me. Jonathan was different, of course. The joke was true — Jonathan Holmes was "a man of the world."

That was what was making me so nervous. Would Jonathan's mother and father find me small-town and boring? What could I talk about? I thought of my sisters, and at that moment I wished for their ability to talk about almost anything to anyone.

I was surprised to find that Jonathan's house was Mom's all-time favorite house in Springwood. For years, she'd been yearning for it.

"Just look at that old beauty," she would say as we walked or drove by the lake. "They don't make them like that anymore."

Jonathan helped me out of the car and took my arm. He led me to a flagstone path that appeared to be newly laid. At least, the dirt was freshly turned, and there was a shovel leaning against a wheelbarrow.

"Practicing," he said. "I've planned a terrace out back. I'll show you later."

I nodded, trying to picture Jonathan at work with a shovel. I guess I had assumed he had gotten his beautiful tan around a pool, or sailing, or some way more glamorous than digging in the dirt. But for some reason I preferred the picture of him working hard, loving what he was doing. I guess it just made him more real to me.

He touched my hair gently. "Too bad you're not two hundred years old," he said.

"What?"

"I told you Mother is crazy about antiques."

I laughed, but now I was nervous again. Was he worried his mother wouldn't like me? Was he nervous?

I looked at him closely as he held the front door open for me. Something had changed in his face. The laughter was gone from his eyes, and his mouth seemed to have narrowed into a expression I had never seen before. Even his manners and the way he spoke had become more formal, even stilted.

I understood his change of mood the minute we entered the spacious front hall and he led me into a huge, high-ceilinged room lined on three sides by bookshelves, which in row after careful row, were filled with handsome, leather-bound books. Jonathan said, "This is the library." But I disagreed silently. The room was too formal, too perfect, too rich to be a library. The word that came to me was "museum." Everything in it was so obviously old and expensive, from the thickly beautiful Oriental rugs, the tasteful arrangement of sofas and ornate chairs and small tables, to the tabletop collections of vases, porcelain figurines, glass, and gold-covered boxes. Just being in the room awed me, made want to speak in a whisper. I loved it. Lucky Jonathan.

"Excuse me for a minute, Colleen," he said. "Let me find my parents and tell them you're here."

I smiled at him, feeling perfectly at ease now. "No hurry," I said, and it was true. He could leave me alone in this beautiful room for hours. It was so peaceful, so perfect, so orderly. It was my kind of place, a fantasy come true.

When he left the room, I looked around more carefully. Even the fire crackling quietly in the marble fireplace was just right, the logs arranged just so, the flames low and controlled, the hearth free of ashes and debris. I compared it with our fireplace in the family room, the wild, loud, super-duper blazes Rory loves to make; the ever-present mess of wood piled against the fieldstone wall, old newspapers, kindling. No such mess here, no noise either. I could hear a pin drop.

Jonathan's father was as tall and handsome as

his son, only older, of course, and without the jaunty eyebrows. He was extremely well dressed. He smoked a pipe, and when he spoke I thought I detected a British accent.

Without intending to, I made comparisons. My own father, on weekends, insisted on wearing his "Comfies" — old khaki trousers and a pilly, red, crewneck sweater with holes in both elbows. For dinner, Dad traded the sweater for a sports shirt, but even then he had the unelegant beginnings of a pot belly. Jonathan's father was the zenith of elegance, just as I'd imagined.

Mrs. Holmes was another story. She was short, plump, and dumpy-looking. Mom would definitely come out on top in any comparison I could come up with. Mrs. Holmes seemed all one color. She had beige hair, beige-ish skin, and she wore a beige skirt, sweater, and shoes. Even her pearl necklace had a yellowish cast to it. She wore absolutely no makeup to brighten up her face. Mrs. Holmes reminded me of the dumplings Dad makes for his famous beef stew — lumpy and bland.

Even her voice was bland. She spoke with very little expression, and a few times I had to strain to hear what she said. I knew I was being mean and critical, but I couldn't help it. I looked from Mr. Holmes to Mrs. Holmes, wondering how such an elegant man had chosen such a wife.

Within a short time, I was really ashamed of those thoughts because she was so sweet to me, really trying to do her best to make me feel at home. It wasn't my mother's warm, lively style of welcome, but I felt Mrs. Holmes's style was just as nice.

"When Jonathan mentioned he'd met a lovely girl at the stables, I insisted on meeting you. It's so important to make nice new friends, I think, don't you?"

"Oh, yes," I agreed. "Very important."

I knew then Jonathan hadn't mentioned how he felt about me. *Why should he?* I thought. I hadn't mentioned Jonathan in my house at all! My family didn't know he existed!

"My son tells me you're a member of the newspaper family. That must be . . . uh . . . interesting. Do you work, too?"

Was it my imagination or was her pale mouth curling in distaste?

"No," I told her. "I guess I'm the only one in the family who isn't active at the paper. Probably because I'm not very talented."

She seemed to like my answer. "Oh, well, my dear, plenty of time to discover what your proper interests are. And newspaper work . . . well, that can be rather a sordid business sometimes."

Her mouth was definitely curling. She wore a look of alarm, as if the whole thing was almost a *dangerous* subject.

"I don't really think the town of Springwood harbors many criminals, Emily," Mr. Holmes said mildly. "I doubt if there is anything you have to worry about."

I was confused, and there was a growing uneasiness in my stomach. Mrs. Holmes appeared older than Mom, but there was something about her, a little girl air, a very small girl afraid of the mean old world. Then she proved it with her next words.

"The world is getting to be such a dreadful place. Even Boston isn't safe anymore. Our house was *robbed* last year." She sighed, and I couldn't help feeling sorry for her. I really wanted to like her.

"I suppose that's why I take such comfort in old things. Everything beautifully crafted and cared for. You didn't see shoddy workmanship in the old days."

That reminded me of Mom's "They don't make them like that anymore," and I told Mrs. Holmes about mother's admiration of her house.

"Well, I'll invite her to tea some afternoon."

She sounded vague and rather disinterested. Maybe I was boring her.

Mr. Holmes and Jonathan had been very quiet, and except for one or two comments, neither of them talked at all. When dinner was over, Mr. Holmes said, "Most enjoyable meal, Emily," but I noticed that he didn't look at his wife when he said it. He was too busy patting his lips with the corner of the white linen napkin.

Actually, it had been a very blah dinner — overdone gristly roast beef, watery mashed potatoes, and canned peas.

Still, except for a few uncomfortable moments, it had been a restful mealtime. *Probably*, I thought, *if I hadn't been there, conversation wouldn't be necessary at all.* If the food were a little better, I decided, I wouldn't mind it at all. It was very different from a Sunday dinner at my house.

Jonathan seemed to perk up then. "Would you excuse us? I want to show Colleen what I'm doing out back."

I could tell Mrs. Holmes didn't approve. "Really, Jonathan, you're not going to start digging again this afternoon, are you? I'm finding earth everywhere. You're tracking so . . ."

"You could take Colleen for a ride in the boat, Jonathan," Mr. Holmes said.

Jonathan didn't have to tell me his parents didn't think much of the work he had chosen. It was very obvious.

As soon as we went outside, though, he did. "Dad expected me to be a lawyer. I told you that. My mother, well, she just can't understand how anyone could possibly enjoy digging around in the earth where worms live."

Jonathan was bitter, and there was no mistaking the fact that he was making fun of his mother. It surprised me. Not once since I'd met him had I heard him say anything mean. Still, I could sympathize. It must be hard to have to do your own thing without encouragement.

He showed me what he had done in the small courtyard by the back door, where the old house jutted out in a long L-shape.

"It might be hard to imagine now," he said eagerly, "but in the spring there will be masses of zinnias and marigolds against the walls and the foundation. In and around the slate, I'm going to plant alyssum, lily-of-the-valley — actually, I planted that last month. September is the ideal month for some of those hardy ground covers such as pachysandra, especially in semi-shaded areas like this . . ."

He grinned suddenly. "You must be fascinated, Colleen. You have to excuse me — I get carried away."

I wrinkled my nose at him. "I know — and you track so."

He laughed, a loud, happy sound. The laughter was back in his eyes, and his mouth was soft again.

"I'll show you some tracking. Come on."

He took my hand and led me down a long slope of leaf-littered grass. We came to the lake's edge and he pulled me quickly behind a huge oak tree. The tree trunk was thick, certainly wide enough to hide us from view in case either of his parents were looking out the window. The family of ducks, a mother and several half-grown children, traveled past us in orderly fashion, not giving us even a quack.

Which was just as well because Jonathan was kissing me and whispering something only I should hear, and the look on his face was meant only for my eyes.

"I love you, Colleen," he said. "Maybe it's too soon, but I do. I love you so."

The late-day sun shone through the bright

leaves overhead and lit his dark skin with spots of gold, and for a moment, I saw him as someone I didn't know.

Then I touched his cheek, and he became Jonathan again.

"I love you, too," I said. "Oh, Jonathan, I do."

Chapter 11

*B*efore Jonathan took me home, we went back in the house so I could say good-bye and thank you. Mrs. Holmes was seated across from her husband, her soft little hands folded neatly in her lap, her head resting on the high back of the chair, her eyes closed. Mr. Holmes, his long, neatly trousered legs stretched out before him on a carved stool, sat with his head back, too, one slender hand draped across his eyes. The FM was playing softly. The strains of some unfamiliar (at least to me) classical music seemed to absorb them completely. They didn't seem to know we were in the room.

How relaxed they are, I thought enviously. What a nice way to spend a Sunday evening. Then I realized they were both asleep!

Jonathan motioned me out of the room. In the hall, he said, "I'll say good-bye for you. I guess I won't try to wake them."

I agreed quickly. "Oh, no, of course not," I

said, and added, "It must be great being an only child, to have so much time for yourself."

"Oh, sure," he said. "Sometimes . . ." He dropped the subject quickly. "What's your favorite flower, Colleen?"

"That's easy," I told him, taking one last look at the gracious, winding staircase, the huge framed portraits of unsmiling Holmeses, the glittering gold and crystal chandelier overhead. "Violets, the kind I see in Hagan's Woods every April."

He held the door for me and smiled. "I should have known. Violets — they suit you."

No, Jonathan, I wanted to say. *I'm a mimosa tree; haven't you noticed?* I was tempted to tell him what Rory said about me being like the shy, shrinking tree, but I decided not to. Just like I hadn't mentioned Dad's garden, even though I knew Jonathan would be interested. That was the point. I didn't want him to get too interested in my family. For as long as possible, I wanted him all to myself.

Naturally, I couldn't *not* let him drive me home, but I could find some way not to invite him in when we got there. I could, and I did.

"I had a wonderful day, Jonathan," I said. "I wish it could last longer, but I'm on duty now. I have to sit with my grandfather."

It might have sounded fine and reasonable to Jonathan, but the instant the words were out of my mouth, I was ashamed. Sit with Grandpa Shawn? I made him sound like a helpless baby. He had to rest a lot, sure, but he was up and around a bit now. I did plan to sit with him, but it was more for my benefit than his.

"He enjoys my company," I explained, hoping that would make up for it. "Sometimes I read to him."

I *didn't* say, "He reads to me, too." Now Grandpa Shawn really sounded like an invalid.

"Hey, that's nice, Colleen," Jonathan said. "Maybe someday you'll read to me. We'll bring a picnic next time we go riding, find a nice spot, and you can read me poetry just like they do in old-fashioned novels."

"Romantic novels, you mean," I said, smiling at him. "You really are very romantic, Jonathan. I suppose it's because you've traveled abroad."

He laughed. "Rub it in. That's okay. I guess I asked for it."

"I like it," I said, and immediately wondered why I liked romanticism in him and was scornful when Maureen mooned over her silly historical romances.

Jonathan started to get out of the car, but I stopped him. "That's okay. I'll just run in now. Thanks a lot, Jonathan. See you tomorrow? Our usual place?"

He sighed and then reached down and captured my hand. "And what else?" he whispered.

I looked into his eyes, and in the dim light I couldn't read them. But I had the feeling that for some reason he was sad, that he didn't want me to leave him.

"What else?" I repeated softly, "What else is — I love you."

"That's better," he said. "Love you, too."

I let him kiss me once. One long, sweet, lingering kiss, and then I got out of the car. Not gracefully, and not very quickly either. His car was so small and low-slung, I had to scramble a lot, unfold my legs, until finally I was standing on the curb looking down at the car.

"Don't forget your bag with your boots," he said suddenly, reaching behind him. He seemed about to get out of the car with it, so I bent over and reached through the window.

"That's okay — thanks," I said hastily. " 'Bye again."

As I watched him pull away from the curb I put my hand up and traced my lips with a finger, remembering his kiss. I turned and walked toward the porch, and as I did I caught a movement from behind the living room curtains. Had someone been watching? Had anyone seen Jonathan's car, seen him kiss me? If so, I was in for lots of questions — the third degree if Maureen or Nora had been looking out the window. I could just hear them.

Slowly, I opened the front door. I shouldn't have been shocked by the sounds of cheerful chatter and laughter, but I was.

Culture shock, I decided as I stood in the doorway. From the tranquillity of Jonathan's house to the beehive I call home.

Hive is right, I thought, seeing one group seated at the dining room table, another bunch huddled in front of the TV, and three more people standing in the hall with me. I recognized a few faces — Nora's friends.

Her actor friends. I learned soon enough we were playing host tonight to the entire cast of *Oklahoma.*

A terrible end to a wonderful day, I thought and sighed deeply. So? What else is new?

I stood still for a while longer, trying to figure how I could make it past the group by the stairs without being noticed. I would go straight up to see Grandpa Shawn and read to him if he wanted me to. I didn't want to be lying to Jonathan. But I had lingered too long; suddenly I had company.

Before I could say a word, a boy had my chin in his hand, and he was turning my face up toward the light.

"Hm-mm, Nora was right," the stranger said. "Classical features, nice eyes. Yes, the eyes are very nice. Nora described you perfectly. She said you . . ."

"Who are you?" I heard myself saying weakly, almost sputtering in my surprise and confusion.

The boy standing very close to me, holding my chin, was medium tall, but he made up for it with masses of curly white-blond hair that stood out at least two inches all over his head. His eyes were a gorgeous shade of blue-green, almost turquoise, and his eyelashes were so long and thick, they appeared to be twin fans. He used them a lot, and when he spoke, every feature seemed to be involved, as if his face were made of rubber.

"Don't you know who I am?" he asked.

"No, I don't think so," I answered slowly.

His rubber face moved into amazed position. "Nora didn't tell you about me? Are you sure? She *said* she did."

Thank heavens he had let go of my chin, for now he made a violent gesture in the air. *"I'm Ronnie Redman."*

Oh, I thought, *him*. The one she said was so "darling," the boy she'd said was so "right" for me *Wrong!* Ronnie Redman was ridiculous. *Let me out of here*, I wanted to say. But I was trapped. Each time I took a step he followed, his arms and face accompanying every word he said. I edged slowly toward the living room.

Nora saw us coming, and she jumped up from the living room floor where she sat with a skinny young man with glasses. She had a ruler in her hand, and she waved it like a magic wand.

"You've already found each other — *perfect!*" she squealed. "Was I telling the truth, Ronnie? Isn't my little sister pretty?"

"Norrr-a," I croaked. How could she do this to me? This had to be the worst.

"Well, someone has to brag about you; you certainly don't."

Ronnie was all stretchy, smiley-face. "I like modesty," he said. "I like shy. You were right, Nora; Colleen is very pretty but better than that, she's not overly talkative. No, not at all. As a matter of fact, I've had to do all the talking."

The skinny boy with glasses looked up and winked at me. "That's a shame, Ronnie. I know it must have been hard for you."

Ronnie ignored him, but I thanked him mentally. This bleached-blond Brillo pad was really getting on my nerves.

"Excuse me," I said, edging toward the kitchen. ". . . glass of water," I mumbled.

He was at my heels. "Me, too," he said. "All that pie made me very thirsty. Colleen, would you please put lots of ice in mine? I like my drinks ice-cold."

"Keep your head in the freezer, Redman," the skinny boy muttered, but when Ronnie glared at him all he did was smile innocently. I could have kissed him. So far, he was my only ally.

Mom and Dad were no help at all. Dad sat, content and unconcerned by the activity swirling around him, alternately reading and watching TV. Mom sat on the floor beside him, her back against his legs, her notebook open and her pen poised. Her eyes were closed. She wasn't asleep, though; I saw her eyelids flip up, and immediately she was scribbling something in her notebook. A few minutes from now, I knew, she'd be reading it to Dad, or whoever would listen. I had no choice. I headed for the kitchen, Ronnie breathing down my neck.

Without speaking, I took ice cubes from the freezer, found tall glasses, and fixed us both ice-water. I felt like telling him to get his own, but thought this would be quicker. Since he thought I was tongue-tied shy, I would play the role. At least it gave me an excuse not to talk to him.

He draped himself over the counter and tried to make eye contact with me, but by now I was so fascinated by the sugar bowl, I couldn't respond. I drank my water slowly.

"What I meant before, Colleen," he began, "is I really do prefer a girl who is quiet and sensible. Being an actor, I need a stabilizing influence, someone who will be there for me . . . through good times and bad, through the successes and failures."

I didn't answer but went on drinking my water.

"From the moment Nora told me about you, I was interested. *Really* interested, Colleen."

I knew I had to look at him some time. I was being horribly rude. But if he expected an "Oh, wow — are you really interested in me?" answer or even a look, he was going to be disappointed.

"Really?" I managed.

The elastic bands allowing him to smile so hugely didn't seem to work so well now. His smile was small and brief. "Oh, I realize how hard it is for anyone to take a backseat, to stay *behind* the scenes, so to speak. But *you* know, having a sister in show business, that there can only be one star per family. The other girls I've gone out with don't seem to understand that. They don't realize how rewarding it can be to . . ."

"Excuse me, Ronnie," I said hastily. "I have to go upstairs."

"Certainly, of course. You'll be right back, though, won't you? I have so much more to tell you."

Unbelievable! I had been going to say I was going upstairs to sit with Grandpa Shawn (the same excuse twice in one night — *oh, great*), but I suppose he just took it for granted I wouldn't excuse myself except for a very urgent reason, the bathroom, of course.

What ego! What nerve! What a dope! One thing, though — it made me feel happier than ever to have Jonathan.

For a minute I thought about going into the downstairs bathroom and staying there until everyone was gone, but that could be hours yet. I was stuck, at least for a while longer. At least until someone came into the kitchen and rescued me. Inwardly I was cursing my training, the family rule that one must be polite to guests, no matter what.

I guess, when I stayed in the room, Ronnie thought he had it made. Any girl who would *suffer* just to stay near him, you know?

The snap returned to his voice and his face. "I really think you're the girl I've been searching for all my life. I just have this feeling. Ever since Nora told . . ."

This time I looked at him when he talked. Partly out of courtesy, but also because something was bothering me, something about his eyes.

All at once, I understood. From where he stood, half-lounging, half-standing, he had a clear view of himself in the glass doors of the dish cabinet directly behind me. I almost choked on the giggle that bubbled up in my throat.

Oh, no, I told myself, desperately trying not to laugh in his face, *he can't be.* I wasn't enough for him, an audience of one was not enough. He had been playing to the cups and saucers, the turkey platter, the salt shaker, and the pepper mill. What a dope! What an absolute fool!

Was I any better? *Who was the bigger fool?* I wondered. *Me, that's who.* Guest or not, he was Nora's friend. And she had no right to match-make behind my back. Maybe she thought she was doing me a big favor. I know she probably meant well, but then she always does. This time I would tell her. This time I wouldn't let her get away with it. Maureen was right; I had to be more assertive. Besides, it was getting harder and harder not to say what I felt, to always push my feelings down. This time . . .

But first I had to deal with the Star. "I think Nora made a mistake. Maybe she didn't tell you."

The corners of his mouth curved down around his chin. "Tell me what?" he asked.

"About my career. Probably because she's so busy with her own."

"Your career? I thought you were still in high school?"

He was alarmed; his face was in spasms.

"I am, but I don't let school hold me back. I only take modeling assignments now, but maybe a film or two . . . soon."

I lifted my chin and held it up toward the light (all by myself) and showed him my profile, first one side, then the other.

"I'm told I'm extremely photogenic. What do you think, Ronnie?"

His "Ohh–hh" gave me the answer to that.

"Well, listen, I have to run now," I said. "It

was great meeting you. Maybe I'll see you again and we can talk shop. I just have to go to bed now . . . beauty sleep. 'Bye."

Instead of hollering at Nora, I should thank her, I thought as I took the stairs two at a time. She had made me angry enough to be really rotten to someone. And with a straight face, too. Wait until I told Grandpa Shawn. That's where I was headed. I hoped he wasn't sleeping, or busy, because now I really did want to be with him. I couldn't wait to tell him what I had just done. I would act it out for him; he would laugh and love it.

I realized I wasn't really angry anymore, not with Nora, not with Ronnie, not with anyone. In fact, I was in a very good mood.

But, I thought very firmly, *she'd better not do that to me again.* Nora didn't know it yet, but I didn't need any fixing up. I didn't need any of her "darling, just right" boys.

I already had one.

Chapter 12

*M*om was at the kitchen table the next morning when I came down. She was still in her bathrobe, drinking coffee. My first class wasn't until nine-twenty, and usually by that time everyone had gone.

"What are you doing home, Mom?" I asked. "Aren't you feeling well?"

She smiled at me. "I'm fine, love. Just thought I'd take a few days off, sort of keep an eye out here. Besides, I've got a week's worth of work done—three features and my column. Leaves me free for a bit."

"That's good," I said.

I knew what she meant. She didn't want to leave Grandpa Shawn home alone.

"He's really getting better fast, isn't he?" I said. "I spent some time with him last night; I had him laughing. He seems like his old self. Grandpa Shawn is something, isn't he, Mom?"

She made a face. "He's something, all right. I keep telling him to watch his diet and not to push the exercise. Dr. Prine told him exactly what to do, and what *not* to do. I have a feeling he didn't listen. Your grandfather has a mind of his own, that's for sure."

I stared at her. I really hadn't spent very much time with him since he'd come home from the hospital. At least, not as much time as I had planned to. I had been too busy thinking about Jonathan, being with Jonathan.

"What do you mean? What's he been doing that he shouldn't be doing?"

"Oh, just little things," she said, exasperation in her voice. "Little things like going up and down all those stairs at least three times yesterday. Little things like snitching potato chips and *two* pieces of your father's deep dish apple pie. I found the empty bag in his wastebasket. Dr. Prine said no heavy, greasy food."

She sighed deeply. "I thought about bringing him down to the first floor, you know, fix up the sewing room for him. But you can imagine how far I got with that idea. He said, and I quote: 'Absolutely not.' "

I could imagine, and also I couldn't really blame him. The "sewing room" isn't a sewing room at all. It's just a dark, gloomy little catch-all room off the kitchen. It's a long way from the spacious, airy, private place on the third floor.

"Grandpa loves his room," I said, and immediately was very angry with him. Why wasn't he following Dr. Prine's orders? Even Grandpa Shawn had admitted his heart attack was a "close call."

"By the way, Colleen," Mom said casually. "Did you have a nice time at your friend's house yesterday? We missed you."

I made my voice just as casual. "Oh sure, very nice. The food wasn't all that terrific, though. I guess I'm just spoiled by Dad's gourmet stuff."

She laughed and took another sip of her coffee. "Where does your friend live?"

Without thinking, I blurted, "Oh, Mom, I was in *your* house. It's beautiful."

Right away I knew I'd made a big mistake.

"*My* house? What do you mean?"

Her blue eyes were wide open and waiting.

"The one on Lake Avenue, the big old white one up on the hill. It's really gorgeous inside. Listen, tell you later. I have to get going."

Now, I thought, *right now before she starts asking more questions.*

"Your friend *lives* in the Holmes house? What's your friend's name?"

"Holmes," I said. It was hopeless.

"Really? Oh, that's exciting. I knew someone had moved in, but I didn't know who. This old newspaper woman must be slipping. How did you meet her? Is she in your school? Now I remember, you said you met her over at Hagan's. Oh, Colleen, I want you to invite her for dinner this coming Sunday. Make sure, I have so many questions about that house. You know, I've always wanted to see the inside. In fact, I've been hoping it would go up for sale. I told your father . . ."

"Mom, I really *have* to go."

"Okay. What's her first name?"

My stomach had begun sinking a few minutes before. Now it had sunk completely. "Who?" I said, stalling for time.

She made a clucking sound and furrowed her forehead. "Your friend, darling. The one we're talking about."

"Jonathan," I muttered. I couldn't out-and-out lie.

"*Jonathan!*" Mom's eyebrows made a dash for her hairline. "I thought you said it was a girl."

I shrugged, trying to look unconcerned. "I didn't say."

Now she grinned and I saw Rory and Patrick and Maureen and Nora all in one.

"Aha!" she said still grinning. "How long has *this* been going on? I thought you were spending more time than usual at Hagan's." She sniffed the air meaningfully. "Do I smell romance?"

"You smell your coffee boiling over," I said. "I've got to go, Mom—right this minute. I'll be late for school."

"Turn the coffee off for me first, will you, love? I'm lazy this morning. It feels so good to be a lady of leisure for a change. Invite him for this Sunday, Colleen. No excuses. I think it's about time we met your friend."

"Okay," I said quietly. "I'll ask him."

I knew I wouldn't get very far arguing with her.

She was being good-natured about it, but underneath the teasing was a family law: Never accept an invitation unless you are prepared to return the favor. No, Jonathan would have to come to dinner whether I liked it or not.

"*Jon-a-than* Holmes," Mom said slowly, rolling the name around on her tongue, repeating it three times, the way she did when she found a new word she liked. "Hmm–mm — nice name. A very Yankee name. If I remember correctly, old Mrs. Holmes had a son who lived in Boston — a lawyer, I believe. So Jonathan must be her grandson."

I nodded. "That's right. He is. Really, Mom — 'bye!"

She smiled and a dreamy expression replaced her amused one. "Did I ever tell you, Colleen, that Boston is my favorite city? In fact, I worked . . ."

"Mom! 'Bye!"

I hurried from the room and the house. *Wait until she hears about London and Switzerland,* I thought. Well, they'd all be hearing soon enough. Poor Jonathan — he's really in for it. And, of course, so was I.

All the way to school, I thought about the Sunday ahead. After that, I knew everything would be changed. And then I had a bad moment during second period, which was English. I felt myself almost hating Mom, and thinking bitterly, *For an old newspaper woman, she's doing just fine — nosy as ever.*

But it wasn't fine for me. The trouble was, I

couldn't blame anyone but myself. I had opened my big mouth and mentioned the old house.

But I knew, even at the beginning, I wouldn't be able to keep Jonathan a secret forever. I had known that, sooner or later, one of them would find out. It was sooner. And it was my tough luck.

All day I was in a really strange mood, not sure whether I wanted to cry or scream. Ms. Charles, my phys. ed. teacher, took me aside and asked me if I wanted to be on the gymnastics team. The team was her idea, and she was all excited about it. I was flattered, and just about to say "yes" when she said: "I've been watching you for a long time, Colleen."

When I thought about it later, I realized she meant she'd been watching my progress on the bars and mats, but at the time she said it, I was really feeling invaded, and it was just the last straw. The very last thing I wanted in this world was anyone watching me.

"No, thanks," I said shortly. "Not interested, Ms. Charles."

She turned away from me then, but not before I saw the puzzlement and hurt in her eyes. "Suit yourself, Colleen."

I felt rotten all during class, and I considered going to her and telling her I had changed my mind. I would apologize, too. Before I could do it, Shari got me really mad. Shari, instead of Ms. Charles, was the last straw. Shari and her busybody mother.

"Guess who my mother's having lunch with today?" Shari said when we were getting dressed after phys. ed.

"I don't know," I muttered, and sighed. I was doing the buttons on my blouse wrong.

"Your boyfriend's mother, that's who — Mrs. Holmes. They're going antiquing afterward. Mom's found a real buddy. Listen, I told her about you liking Jonathan, and so she's going to find out all she can about him. I told Mom to find out if he . . ."

I felt the button between my fingers for a split second and then heard it chink-chink against the tile locker room floor.

"Oh, now look what you did," Shari said giggling. "Now're you're in big trouble."

The button belonged halfway down — the worst possible spot.

The words tumbled out so fierce and hard, I almost couldn't believe it was my voice. "No, Shari — look what *you* did. *You* are the big trouble! Why don't you mind your own business? I don't need you or your mother spying for me or *on* me. Don't you two have anything better to do than prying into other people's lives? You have no right!"

Shari was staring at me, her brown eyes huge with shock. "Colleen," she gasped. "I didn't mean . ."

"Oh, no, you didn't *mean*," I said nastily. "Everyone always means well — I'm so sick of it."

Her face was white, and she held herself very straight. "I don't understand. I thought it would be fun. I was trying to help . . . as a . . ." Her voice broke. "As a friend."

"I don't need any help, Shari," I said coldly. "Just leave me alone from now on."

I had never ever been this nasty to anyone in my life. I hadn't known I was capable of it. I knew it now. So did Shari. She gave me one last bewildered look and turned away. She gathered up her books and walked off.

I was wrong — I *did* need help. I had to ask Ms. Charles if I could use the sewing kit kept for emergencies. Everyone else had gone on to their next class. We were alone. I felt shaky and confused, and I looked at her hard, wanting to say something to change the horrible silence between us. Maybe if I talked to her, told her about the way I felt, explained . . .

But I couldn't. And it took me a long time to sew on the dumb button. My hands were so shaky, I couldn't seem to thread the needle. Then, because it was so late, I had to ask for a slip to get me into my next class. She didn't look at me, and I knew Shari wasn't going to be my friend ever again either.

But why should I feel so guilty? I wondered. My anger came back to help me. I shouldn't feel bad about what I'd said to Shari. She deserved it, didn't she? Miss Information Booth had had it coming for a long time. Imagine Mrs. Brubaker discussing me and Jonathan with Mrs. Holmes! Lunch. I hoped her soup was cold and her hamburger was raw. Maybe the waiter would drop the salad in her lap.

It was a bad day. The worst. Then I remembered — it wasn't over yet. The worst was still to come. On Sunday.

Chapter 13

$\mathcal{M}$om surprised me. She didn't make any dramatic announcements about my "friend" until she absolutely had to, which was on Sunday when Mom, Patrick, and I were setting the table.

"How many plates today, Mom?" Patrick asked. "Anyone coming?"

Mom was rubbing at a spot on the green linen tablecloth.

"Just one extra," she murmured. "Colleen's guest — Jonathan Holmes."

I pretended to be very busy selecting silverware, but I could feel Patrick's stare, I could feel his grin. *Here it comes,* I thought. *Ready or not.* I'd had all week to prepare for just this kind of thing, but was I ready? No!

"No kidding?" Patrick's voice came out like it used to before it changed a few years ago, high-pitched and squealy. He moved over to stand beside me, and then almost turned his head upside down so he could look into my face.

"Colleen? No kidding?"

I tried to smile. Probably I just looked nauseous. "No kidding, Patrick."

His thump on my back was followed by a hug that was pure Kelly Bear. "Hey, that's great, Little Sister. Don't you think, Mom? I'd say it was about time, too."

If I kept a straight face, it was not without effort. Stay calm, I told myself — get it over with.

Now Patrick had his hands on his hips, and he wore a fierce scowl. "This guy better be pretty darned decent," he said. (Decent is Patrick's current word.)

"Oh, Patrick, for heaven's sake," Mom said, frowning.

I could tell, though, that most of her attention was centered on the rather sad collection of mums she'd salvaged from the garden. As I watched, she pulled one flower out of the vase altogether, and viewed those remaining with a critical eye.

"Give your sister some credit, please," she said, fixing Patrick with the same look. "Anyone Colleen likes enough to invite to dinner would have to be — as you say — decent."

Patrick relaxed his macho pose and grinned. "Okay. Well, just checking."

He lifted a pile of dinner plates and began dealing them out. "You *really* like him, Colleen? This guy — Jonathan Holmes?"

Keep calm, I thought. *Get in practice for Maureen and Nora.*

"Yes," I said. "He's nice." I waited a few seconds and added, "It's really no big thing."

Maybe that would squelch him a little. It didn't.

"What are you talking about — of course, it's a big thing. It's the first guy you've had over to meet the family."

He put on a woebegone face. "Naturally, I'm always the last to know about these things."

"Actually, you're the second to know," I said. "Mom knew first."

"Yes," Mom said. "Although I had to wring it out of you. Now I'm dying to meet him. What time did you tell him, Colleen?"

"Four," I said, and sighed. "It's twenty of."

"Well, don't sweat it, sis," Patrick said. "I, for one, will be on my best behavior."

He grinned again and pinched my cheek. "So you're in love . . . finally. That's good — you're too cute to be a wallflower all your life."

Mom folded the last napkin and flashed Patrick another look.

"Colleen is not now, nor has she ever been a wallflower," she said indignantly. "She's just very choosy. Nothing wrong with that."

Patrick put both hands up and backed away. "Sorry," he said. "No offense."

I was more amazed than offended at that moment. I was thinking how much Patrick had changed, from cute but ornery, insulting, and hard-to-live-with, to warm, happy, affectionate, and handsome. My brother was all grown up, full of self-confidence. I really was very fond of him. I just hoped that shortly before Jonathan arrived, Patrick would get a severe case of lockjaw.

"Colleen, love, check with your father," Mom

said. "Find out what serving dishes he's going to need."

On Sunday, Mom wasn't allowed in the kitchen, because as Dad put it, "Your Mother can't keep her opinions to herself." Even Mom admitted she could be a nuisance.

I left the room gratefully. One down, five to go: Dad, Rory, Maureen, Nora, and Grandpa Shawn. Mom said he insisted on having dinner downstairs today, and "From now on!"

At breakfast, Mom repeated Grandpa Shawn's speech, word for word.

"Maggie, darlin'," he'd said to Mom, "It's about time I had some real food on my tongue, and a good hearty taste of my family, too."

Grandpa Shawn was the least of my worries. I had thought about telling him about Jonathan, but I hadn't. I guess I was just stretching out the privilege of having Jonathan all to myself. Soon enough, he would pass into "the public domain" or rather, "the Kelly domain."

After I consulted with "The Chef" and passed the word to Mom, I glanced at the clock and ducked into the downstairs bathroom. Dad had given me a four-thirty sit-down deadline which would allow plenty of time for introductions.

"I hope he's punctual," Dad said when I informed him I had a guest coming for dinner. "Potatoes au Brian must be served piping hot."

At least Jonathan would have a good meal, I thought as I fluffed my hair and examined my face. Dad's potatoes au Brian only looked mashed — several top-secret ingredients made them special. Plus, I noticed, he'd made his fabulous apple stuffing for the big pork roast.

It had been Wednesday before I got around to inviting Jonathan. He'd said yes right away, and ever since, he'd been asking me questions about my family. I couldn't blame him. After all, he knew only that my folks were *The Sun* people. He knew my grandfather was recovering from a heart attack. He knew Samson, and he knew me. Not too much to go on, I suppose, if you want to be prepared, to feel at ease. But I'd evaded all of his questions.

Besides, I had thought, *he'd find out for himself soon enough.* Not that I thought he'd hate them or anything. But since Jonathan was so low key and quiet, I was afraid he would think they were . . . well, just kind of . . . too much.

I was worried for him, but the real truth was I was worried for myself, too. I kept thinking that my beautiful secret wouldn't be secret anymore, that my personal life would stop being personal.

Jonathan wouldn't get off easy. Before they got through with him, they'd know who his first-grade teacher was, whether he liked disco or rock, if he supported the ERA, and did he dream in color or black and white.

I paced the front hall and waited for the doorbell to ring, alternating between two silent prayers. The first was: *Please Jonathan, be on time. Let's get this over with.* The other one was: *Please, Jonathan, call now and say you can't make it. Say your mother grounded you for tracking earth in on her Oriental rug.*

In other words, I was slightly hysterical, and maybe that's why when the doorbell rang and I opened the door the first thing I said to Jonathan was, "Don't worry — we have wall-to-wall — and it's six years old."

No wonder he looked startled and uneasy.

At that very moment, Patrick burst into the front hall. "Well, let the poor guy in, Colleen," he said, rolling his eyes toward heaven. "Some hostess *you* are!"

My brother stepped forward, first shook Jonathan's hand, then yanked him forward, leading him quickly toward the dining room.

"Good thing I came along when I did, Jonathan," Patrick said in a real buddy-buddy voice. "If you waited for *her*, you'd probably miss dinner altogether. Which would be a terrible shame because our father is the best cook in the world, or at least, in Central Jersey."

Now Patrick's voice sank to a loud whisper. "Give you one good tip, though. If you really hate something you find on your plate, try at least one bite. Dad goes absolutely berserk if you don't at least try something he's slaved over. You can't fake it either, right, Colleen? Dad watches you chew!"

I groaned. "Patrick," I said. "Stop — don't scare him to death!"

Jonathan looked over at me, and gave me a half-smile. "Don't worry, Colleen. I'm a very good chewer. I've had lots of practice."

I thought of last Sunday's dry, gristly roast beef.

"As a matter of fact," he continued seriously,

"I'm a champion chewer. I have the annual Charleston Chew medal to prove it."

Patrick stared at Jonathan for a minute and then burst out laughing. "Hey, Jonathan, can you do liver?"

I looked at Patrick, then at Jonathan. He seemed to grow pale under his tan. "Are we . . . having liver . . . today?"

Patrick laughed. "Just like me. Can you beat it, Colleen? He hates liver, too. Remember my liver rebellions? I kept getting sent to my room, but you and Nora always snuck me in cheese sandwiches and jars of olives."

I turned to Jonathan. "Don't worry," I said. "We're not having liver today."

His eyes turned cloudy as he looked at me. His lips were pressed together so his mouth was just a long, straight line. "I'm not worried, Colleen," he said softly. "So don't *you* worry."

He seemed impatient with me, as if I were getting in his way, spoiling his fun or something. Then he smiled at me, and the clouds lifted, and I knew I was just being silly. In his eyes now, there was a clear message for me: I read: "I love you, Colleen." I felt myself relax.

Mom swept into the dining room, her face and hair warm and radiant. She had a covered dish in one hand and a single yellow mum in the other.

"I found one more," she said triumphantly, handing the flower to Jonathan. "Put it in the vase with the others, love, then let me have a good look at you. I'm hoping there'll be a family resemblance. I knew your grandmother. Did you know that?"

Jonathan's face was bright, too, as he placed the flower carefully in the green and white vase. Not blushing-bright or embarrassed. Jonathan looked very pleased — *happy*!

I felt a pang of envy mixed with wonder. How had Mom known the perfect thing to do? Hand him the flower? The gesture was just so right! Come to think of it, how had Patrick hit upon the one food-hate he shared with Jonathan? How did they always manage to be so darned charming?

It was just as I thought. In just a few minutes, Jonathan was already "one of the family" — not mine anymore.

But I did expect it, didn't I? I should have known that in this family there can never be any such thing as "mine." Everything, every place, every*one* has to be "ours," shared.

Jonathan was laughing now at something Mom was telling him. His perfect white teeth were flashing, and his glossy dark hair made the perfect frame for his fine-boned face. But at that moment, the admiration I saw in his eyes wasn't directed at me. Not his smile either.

I remembered what Jonathan said a few minutes earlier. ". . . don't *you* worry, Colleen."

All right, so I wouldn't worry. After all, why should I? Everything was going well; Jonathan seemed to be enjoying himself. I should be happy.

Chapter 14

*M*aureen and Rory appeared at the exact moment Dad's first fanfare sounded from behind the closed kitchen door. They took their seats at the dining room table, nodding, smiling, but strangely silent. Jonathan looked up and I saw his eyes widen as the voice-trumpet sounded for the second time.

"Da da da *dut* de dah!"

The door swung open, and Dad entered in grand style carrying a steaming platter in his hands. His face was flushed red with kitchen heat and pride, and he wore his "Aloha" shirt, the one he bought at the National Newspaper Publishers Association convention in Honolulu. A happy Hawaiian king, I decided, bearing his crown of pork.

He set the platter down with a flourish, and as he did he looked straight at Jonathan and said (as if he'd known him all his life): "How's that? Looks pretty good, doesn't it?"

Before Jonathan could say anything, Grandpa Shawn made his entrance. He really did look splendid in his favorite burgundy sports jacket, white shirt, and striped tie. His hair and mustache glistened silver, and his eyes seemed bluer than usual.

"Brian, me boy," he said, rolling the words on his tongue. "Sure, and you are your dear departed mother's pride and joy and my own heart's delight. The perfume of this sumptuous repast reaches to heaven itself."

He threw back his head, closed his eyes, and sighed blissfully.

Oh, no, I was groaning silently. Not his County Mayo act, not right off the bat. At least let Jonathan see him as the dignified, highly intelligent, interesting person he really is, before he sees the ultra-Irish act. I could only hope he wouldn't keep it up, maybe singing a chorus or two of "The Irish Soldier Boy," or his favorite, "When Your Old Wedding Ring Was New." I could just imagine how Jonathan was seeing this scene.

Grandpa Shawn spotted Jonathan, reached across the table, and shook his hand. Watching, I saw a small smile begin at the corners of Jonathan's mouth.

"I was just going to say the same thing myself, sir."

I didn't have to look at Grandpa Shawn's face or at any of the others to know Jonathan had scored a hit. The general burst of delighted laughter made it obvious.

And I thought he would be demolished by my

family? Why, he was a pro—smooth and cool as silk. *How well did I know him,* I wondered.

Maureen got up from her chair, went to the doorway, and peered out. I heard her muffled "Hurry up, Nor . . ."

Maureen returned to her seat, and was just giving Jonathan one of her best Miss New Jersey smiles, when Nora, or someone, shuffled in. All talk stopped mid-sentence.

The source of the shuffling sound was her soft, embroidered slippers on the hardwood floor that begins where the wall-to-wall ends. But the exotic slippers and the strange mincey walk were small stuff compared to the rest of her.

Nora's face was powdered stark white, her mouth a slash of scarlet, her brows and all around her eyes traced with jet black. Her long hair in a loose upsweep was stabbed twice through with black enamel chopsticks, and a long red silk kimono was wrapped at the waist with black silk. Her head was bowed, her white eyelids lowered demurely, the tips of her fingers pressed together under her chin.

Oh, stop, I protested inwardly. *Not today!*

She bowed, not once but several times.

Dad's amused smile vanished, and he waved Nora to her chair. "Will you please stop all this bobbing up and down and let us get on with dinner? Everything's going to be ice cold!"

Actually, the questions for Nora were brief and few. "What's *this* getup for?" "Where'd you find the neat slippers?" and "Are those the chopsticks I bought in Chinatown last year?" No one seemed a bit surprised, or even impressed with having a geisha girl at Sunday dinner. To tell the truth, on any other day I wouldn't have blinked an eye either. We were all used to Nora's costumes, her entrances, the game of Dress Up she'd played since she was a very little girl. I knew the outfit could be her costume for a new play, or something she had spent the morning doing just for fun.

As the passing and serving of food took everyone's attention, I stole a look at Jonathan. He seemed very calm and cool, as if he were perfectly used to having dinner with a family that included a Hawaiian, an Irish poet, and a redheaded Japanese girl.

He was holding his own in the general conversation, answering questions about his house, his travels, his schooling. At the moment he was describing Crofton, the "public" school he'd attended just outside London.

"Over there public means private," he explained. "Here, I guess, it would be prep."

"Hmm-mm," Maureen said, narrowing her eyes and furrowing her forehead in the same way Mom does. "You *do* have a definite preppie look, Jonathan. We don't see that very much in Springwood. It's not just the way you dress, or speak, or act. It's something more subtle . . . an *essence*."

She paused for quite a long time, but I could see her revving up for one of her favorite serious discussions about "essence." *If Maureen could have her way,* I thought grimly, *every new person who came her way would walk away with a door prize — a hardbound, gilt-edged copy of* The World According To Maureen Kelly *by Maureen Kelly*. That and the fond memory of her tawny hair and fabulous smile. Because she wanted it both ways: Love my mind, but tell me how beautiful I am.

A second later, I was ashamed. Why was I being so hard on Maureen? Why was I sitting here like a sulky lump, thinking mean things and being miserable? No one said I couldn't be part of it all — the talk, the fun, the family. Actually, I should be happy, thrilled, that the boy I loved was making such a big hit. More than that, I should be happy that *he* was having such a great time. And, of course, he was. Jonathan's gray eyes were truthful reporters, clouds or clear weather, a cinch to read.

I caught Dad saying, "What will you be preparing for, Jonathan?"

The minute Jonathan said the words landscape architect and went on to tell him a few of his ideas for beautifying Springwood, I knew he was in like Flynn. It also meant I was going to have to share him for a while longer.

"Right after dinner, we'll take a walk out back, Jonathan," Dad said. "I'd like you to see my compost setup."

"Don't forget, Jonathan," Mom said leaning toward him, "I want you to see the article Maureen wrote about Holmes House, I mean, *your* house. And tomorrow, when I go to the office, I'll make a copy for you."

And so on. And so forth.

Even Patrick said, "Don't forget later, Jonathan." That puzzled me. Had I missed something? Probably. Thinking can make me deaf to the world.

As I helped clear the table, I decided that as soon as I decently could, I was going to kidnap Jonathan, take him to Hagan's before the daylight was all gone. It was getting dark very early now, and colder. I'd have to talk to Jonathan about changing our riding times. Maybe he could pick me up right after school or something. But I would have to wait. Right now, Dad and Jonathan and Rory were leaving the table.

"Excuse us, everyone, we'll have our dessert later," Dad said. "Grasshopper pie, so all of you begin right now to anticipate."

The fluffy green pie is one of Dad's greatest concoctions, made with *creme de menthe* and topped with shaved chocolate. When I saw Jonathan's eyes light up at the mention of pie, I groaned silently. It didn't look now as if he were going to have time to squeeze me into his busy schedule. I was going to be lucky if I got to say good-bye. *Forget about a good night kiss,* I thought bitterly.

Chapter 15

"*Y*ou don't want to play poker?" Jonathan asked. "Why not, Colleen?"

He looked honestly puzzled and, it seemed to me, kind of disapproving.

"I'm not much of a card player, that's why," I said. "I thought . . ."

He interrupted me. "Oh, come on. It will be fun. I haven't been in a good game since, well, since Crofton, I guess."

He threw his head back and laughed. (Had he always laughed so loud?) "I was telling Patrick about the time" — Jonathan stopped talking to laugh again — " the time I lost my shirt, I mean, literally, Colleen. I bet my shirt and I lost it to a pair of ladies."

I looked at him. Could I really have been so wrong about him?

"You lost your shirt to some ladies? That's cute." My voice sounded freezing cold even to me. It stopped him short. He stared at me. Then he laughed again, louder than ever.

"You're really telling the truth about not being a card player," he said. "Colleen, sweetheart, ladies are queens." He cocked his head. "You know — queens in a pack of cards."

He was frowning a little, probably thinking I was very dumb as well as not very much fun. But his frown disappeared and he was smiling at me. "Come on, Colleen — smile." His voice was soft, gentle.

"I thought we might go to Hagan's for a while," I said. "Just you and me. Give Samson and Black Satin a few minutes together, too. We have time. It's not dark yet."

"Oh, let's not," he said. "Not today. We can ride anytime, and I already promised Patrick I'd play. If you don't feel like playing, just sit beside me for luck."

He put both hands on my shoulders and looked deep into my eyes. "Please?"

I wouldn't smile. He could just brush off riding, being alone with me, with a casual "We can do that anytime."

He thought so, huh? "Sit beside me," "Bring me luck." Did I look like a rabbit's foot?

"You play," I said, pulling away from him. "I'm really not interested in the game."

Or you either, I wanted to say. At least not the way you are now: so hyper and hectic, talking up a storm, laughing all the time, making points all over the place. I had been interested in, loved, the

Jonathan with the soft voice, the slow, sweet smile, the boy who understood my need to take things easy, to be quiet. Today, though, Jonathan could be a carbon copy of Rory or Patrick; loveable, handsome, but on all the time, bursting with energy, noisy.

"We're waiting for you," Nora trilled from the family room. "Dealer's choice, Jonathan, and you're the first dealer."

Jonathan turned and walked toward the room so fast, I had no choice but to follow him. Patrick, Nora, and Rory were already sitting at the game table and Dad already had the TV going, and the book review section open on his lap. Maureen was sitting on the floor with a huge pile of newspapers beside her.

Nora looked at me. "Are you playing, Colleen?" she asked.

"No," I said, watching as Jonathan sat down, picked up the deck of cards, and began shuffling.

"I didn't think so," she said. "Sit with us, though. Maybe you'll bring Jonathan some luck."

Nora had washed her face clean of the white powder and let her hair loose, but she still wore the red silk kimono. She looked really pretty.

Patrick snorted. "Luck — he'll need it. Did you hear Jonathan always loses his shirt? I think we got ourselves a victim, folks."

"You think so, huh?" Jonathan said indignantly. "Well, tonight I'm a winner. I feel it."

"We'll see," Rory said.

Maureen glanced up from where she sat in a

nest of newspapers. She smiled slyly. "Nice shirt you're wearing, Jonathan."

"Yeah," Patrick agreed. "Wonder how it's going to look on me."

Nora giggled. "Or me. I look pretty good in shirts like that. Ask Rory. I borrow his all the time."

"Steal, you mean, Nora. In fact, do you have my new blue one? I can't find it."

"Well, don't worry about it, Rory," Patrick said. "Chances are you'll win Jonathan's tonight."

Jonathan laughed, a wicked sound, mocking. "Don't worry about me," he said, and began dealing the cards.

"Uh oh," Maureen said, not looking up. "Watch out, you guys. I have a feeling Jonathan means business."

I stared at the back of his head. He was sitting with his shoulders hunched, his head bent, the cards almost flying as he dealt them. He did seem to know what he was doing.

It was also very clear that he had forgotten all about me. All he cared about was winning this stupid card game.

I walked out of the family room and no one noticed. I went in to the kitchen, found Mom talking to her friend Cookie on the phone. I stood there, waiting for her, and finally she told Cookie "Just a moment," and asked me what I wanted.

"Would you do me a favor?" I said. "Tell Jonathan I wasn't feeling well, and I went up to lie down. He's hot into poker right now, and I hate to spoil his fun. If I feel better, I'll come down. If not . . ."

"Go ahead, love. I'll tell him. If you fall asleep, I'm sure he'll understand."

"Thanks, Mom."

"Colleen?" There was a dreamy look in her eye.

"Yes, Mom?"

"Jonathan's terrific. You have good taste."

"Mmm-mm," I murmured, and left the room, glad she was still on the phone, and I didn't have to talk about him any more than that.

Grandpa Shawn had gone up to his room shortly after dinner, saying he was going to write for a while. "You all have inspired me," he had said.

I would go up and ask him if I could sit with him. We could talk or not talk; it didn't really matter. What did matter was knowing he truly loved me. I wasn't sure anymore about Jonathan. After today, I wasn't sure at all.

The door was open. Grandpa Shawn was sitting at his desk leaning on his elbows, his chin propped in his hands. The desk lamp was on, making one large golden circle around him like a spotlight. He could have been an actor, alone on a stage, the audience silently watching from the shadows. The audience — me.

I watched him for a long moment, wondering what he was dreaming about. His eyes were open, but he had to be very far away. Somewhere far and really nice, I thought, because he looks so happy, so serene.

"You're so lucky, Grandpa Shawn. Do you know that?"

I wanted to say that, and then to ask: "Tell me how to be the way you are. Tell me because I need to know now before things get any worse. I need to know and I need this room because it's the only place left. Hagan's Woods are spoiled for me now. The woods will be full of Jonathan even when I'm alone. I will be thinking about him, seeing his face, listening for his breathing, and the sound of Black Satin's hoofs behind me. I need this room where Jonathan has never been, and the blue chair." Most of all I wanted to say: "And you, Grandpa Shawn, I need you. Help me please. Show me what to do. Tell who I am."

But I knew I couldn't say one word of it. Dr. Prine had said, "No upsets, no extra stress." *Maybe someday,* I thought, when he's stronger; not now.

Finally I rapped lightly on the open door. "Hi," I said. "You busy?"

He looked up, blinked a few times, and his eyes searched the shadows beyond his golden circle. "Is that you, Collie? Come in, darlin'. Come over here where I can see you."

I stretched my lips so tight over my teeth, the corners of my mouth hurt, but it's a smile, I thought — the best I can manage. Someday I would ask Maureen if the corners of her mouth ever hurt? But I answered the question for myself as I crossed the room to Grandpa Shawn. No,

Maureen would have said so; she would already have discussed at length the problems of smiling. I stopped walking and stood just outside the circle of light.

I would have to talk to Grandpa Shawn now. I would have to be cheerful and not let him know the truth. I certainly couldn't talk about Shari, or Jonathan, or the family. I couldn't ask him, "Tell me something, Grandpa Shawn. Why does every one else in the world want the volume turned up, the music louder, and I can't wait to turn it down? Why am I so different? What's wrong with me?"

"Is something wrong, darlin'? Why, of course there is. You're crying. Collie, come over here to me." But instead, he got up from his desk and came to me.

"I'm not really crying, Grandpa Shawn. I'm just . . ."

"No, you're not crying. You're sobbing. Ah, my darlin' girl, tell me. Tell Grandpa." He had his arms around me. He hugged me to his chest.

"You're not supposed to get upset," I whimpered. "You shouldn't . . ."

"Yes, I should," he said very firmly. "And I'm glad you came up to me. It's nice to be needed, you know."

"I do," I said. "Oh, you don't know how much I need you. I'm so confused, I'm so worried."

"Worry here, Collie," he said, and led me to the blue chair.

He sat me down, then pulled the old brown leather hassock close to the chair. He sat there beside me and lifted one of my hands and pressed it between his own. He kissed my fingers one by one (two kisses for the pinkie), the way he used to do when I was little.

"Now, Collie, tell me. And take your time. Whatever it is, don't hurry the telling. I have all the time in the world."

The tears were still coming but slower now. Being in the chair with Grandpa Shawn close beside me took away most of the panicky feeling. Maybe I would be able to tell him.

"I was going to tell you about Jonathan quite a while ago. But then, a part of me didn't want to tell anyone. Not even you."

"If you talked about him, Collie, he wouldn't be the same, would he? He wouldn't be just yours to think about privately. He'd be more like the photo of Samson you took one day, all by yourself with Patrick's hand-me-down camera. The photo you sent out to be developed and then framed so carefully. And then because it was such a beautiful picture, you had to bring it out to show every time company came. Is that it, darlin'? You didn't want the same thing to happen with your Jonathan?"

"Yes," I said gratefully.

How did he know it so exactly — and I knew only parts of it — that I resented the way my sisters moved Samson's photo, burying it under their clutter, making me search for it all the time, and Mom telling the same old story: "Samson's such a brute, but so gentle, really . . ." making my horse, my picture, a part of the family's show and tell.

"Yes, that's it, Grandpa Shawn. And I think I'm afraid, too."

"Afraid of what?" His voice was soft in the semi-darkness, and his hands felt warm and dry around mine.

"That Jonathan would discover that I was kind of . . . dull. Next to them, I mean.

"Them?"

"Oh, all of you," I said impatiently, sniffling a little. "You're all so smart and bright and talented and more colorful than I am. You all shine, and I don't. I thought Jonathan would see the difference, would see that I'm different, and he did, Grandpa Shawn. That's exactly what happened today. I discovered something, too. Jonathan isn't who I thought he was, not who I want him to be. Somehow, it's all just spoiled."

I sat there for a minute thinking about what I had just said. Then I looked up and met Grandpa Shawn's gaze directly. "I don't know what to do." A tear plopped on Grandpa Shawn's hand but neither of us wiped it away.

"What would you like to know how to do, Collie?" he prodded gently. "Maybe I can help you with it."

"It's hard to explain," I said. "I sound so whiny even to myself. It's just that I feel so crowded in all the time. There's always so much going on here. So many people bunched together in one room but filling every room. Sometimes I need to get away from it and I look around and there's no place I can go. I get so frustrated, and that makes me be mean, makes me think mean thoughts. I hurt a friend of mine the other day. I insulted my favorite teacher, too. I hated myself later."

I told him about having to hide out in the bathroom and about Ronnie Redman. I told him all about Jonathan and how his face looked when he kissed me last week behind the big tree. I described Mr. and Mrs. Holmes and the beautiful house, the portraits on the wall, the thick Oriental rug, all creamy and beautiful blue and apricot. I talked on and on, barely stopping for breath, and Grandpa Shawn sat there very quietly, his blue eyes intent on my face, holding my hand and listening.

Even as I said the last few words, I remembered the evening he had offered me a penny for my thoughts and I refused. *I'm really making up for it now,* I thought. At last I ran out of words and breath and I stopped. I swallowed hard.

"Don't move, Collie," Grandpa Shawn said, getting up, placing my hand back on my lap. "I'll be back in a jiffy."

I sat very still. I was very tired and I felt numb. I knew my legs and feet had fallen asleep already.

He returned with a can of orange soda in one hand and his bathroom glass in the other.

"Shall we share?" he said, his eyes twinkling. "But don't tell on me. According to Dr. Prine, I should avoid all carbonated drinks. I'm becoming a very devious character, Collie, raiding the kitchen like a thief every night. Tell you the truth, darlin', I kind of like the sneaky life, keeps me on my toes."

I drank the sweet orange stuff greedily.

"Now, then . . ." He took the empty can from my hand and put it down beside his glass on the small round table. "Collie, I want to explain something to you. Something I think might be just the ticket. It worked for me and I think maybe it will work for you."

His eyes searched mine for a moment. "Collie, are you able to picture things in your mind? Are you able to hold a picture steady, look at it, see it clearly?"

He didn't wait for my answer.

"It's called 'imaging,' forming a clear image in order to consider it even after the event or person or place has gone or has been taken away. Can you do that, Collie?"

I thought of how I had done just that after I met Jonathan, how fuzzy and vague he was at first until I found the time to work on it, and now his face was so perfectly clear in my mind. I had done it with other faces, other things, for as long as I can remember.

"Yes," I said. "I do it all the time."

"That's fine, Collie. Just what I hoped."

"Why?" I asked. "What's so good about it? It's not such a big deal. I mean, it's not a talent."

"Yes, it is," he said. He leaned toward me, fixing me with his bright eyes. "This room — you like it, don't you, darlin'?"

"I like it a lot," I said. "I love it."

"And this old chair you're sitting in . . . you love it, too, don't you?"

"Right," I agreed. "I like to curl up in it even

though my feet always go to sleep. Like now."

He ignored that. "And the lovely Chinese rug you saw at Jonathan's house, and the elegant marble fireplace. Wouldn't the rug and the fireplace do wonders for this room?"

I was intrigued now but puzzled. What was he doing?

"Yes, but . . ."

"And these windows across the front here. You can see the tops of the trees."

"I even like the branches without leaves," I said. "Even in winter."

"Wouldn't you like to have a room like this room but with improvements? Your own special touches? A room where no one ever comes except you? A strictly private room?"

"Sure," I said, frowning now. I had always wanted my own room. "But what . . . ?"

"No one could meddle with your things, misplace your belongings. There could be a special shelf for Samson's photo, and you could have music . . . or not. Lights on . . . or not. You could furnish it, keep it just as you want it, and no one could ever take it away from you. Wouldn't that be nice, darlin'?"

"It would, Grandpa Shawn, but . . ."

"Collie, if you can image properly, then you can have that room.

"I've had this room and the room I imaged years ago," he said. "Not everyone is lucky enough to have two ivory towers amid the treetops. But you can have at least one room, a place to go, a door to shut on all the noise and the clamor. Go there, rest, and then return to your life refreshed."

Could I? Really? I guess he saw the doubts in my eyes.

"I've lived a long time, darlin', and during most of those years, I was traveling, writing, living out of suitcases, always on the move, usually with a crowd around me, or people anyway. Sometimes it felt like I was never alone. I found myself in the damnedest situations with the damnedest people. Even in New York, at the paper, there were people, typewriters, machines clattering, and if I hadn't had that quiet little room in my head to retreat to, I doubt if I would have lived this long or this happily."

He smiled. "That's what you need, my Collie, some quiet place to go and rest your pretty head."

I sat very still and closed my eyes. Fuzzy around the edges, wavering and indistinct like an old mirror, a picture was forming in my mind. I caught a glimpse of the outlines of a chair. I sensed there was a fire burning, a tidy fire, the hearth clean, a low table, pictures on the walls.

I kept my eyes closed. "Grandpa Shawn," I whispered, "I think I can do it!"

I opened my eyes and stared at him. "It works!"

He squeezed my hand. "It will take some time to make it just right for you. And, of course, you can add to it over the years, change it as *you* change.

"Feel free to take whatever you need from *this* room — be my guest. Definitely this old chair. And just think, darlin', rent-free. Best of all, portable. You can take it with you everywhere you go."

My legs weren't numb anymore; they hurt. I had to get up. I told Grandpa Shawn.

"Here," he said, rising from the hassock, bending over me. "Let me help you get untwisted here."

"I love you," I said, putting my arms around his neck, burying my face in the soft fine wool of his robe. "You always make me feel better. I'm going to try what you said. I think it will help."

I was suddenly very, very sleepy. "Can we talk some more tomorrow?"

He kissed the side of my face and brushed my hair with his hand. "You're tired, sweet girl. It's been a hard day for you, I know. But just one more thing — a *warning*."

I waited, my head on his shoulder.

"Once you have your room, use it sparingly. Go there when you have to, even when you want to, but don't stay in it too much. Don't lock the door. Because crazy as it can be sometimes, the world is beautiful, too. You need both, Collie, the world, people, doing things, going places, living fully, *and* a quiet place to go, too. Both, darlin'. Remember that."

"I won't forget, Grandpa Shawn," I said. My legs were pins and needles and I hopped up and down, stamping my feet, shaking my legs.

"I haven't seen you do that for a long time," he said. "You bring back memories of the old Collie, the little girl Collie."

"Tomorrow, okay?" I said as I left his room.

"We'll talk some more tomorrow."

He didn't answer, just smiled and blew me a kiss.

It took only minutes to get undressed and into bed and only seconds, I think, to fall asleep.

Chapter 16

*I*n study hall the next morning, I practiced imaging my room. It was still blurry, and I couldn't decide whether the windows should look out on treetops, or if an ocean view would be nicer. I would work on it, I decided — take my time, make it perfect.

In phys. ed. I didn't actually speak to Shari, but once when she looked at me, I smiled, and the second time she looked my way I made a tragic face, the way Patrick does when he wants to say "I'm sorry."

I smiled at Ms. Charles, too, but I really don't think she saw me. I think she was watching someone else at the parallel bars.

I felt much better. Partly because of the good night's sleep, and mostly because of Grandpa Shawn. He had really come through for me.

Just after lunch, during history, the squawk box above Mrs. Bruno's desk came to staticky life. "Colleen Kelly to the main office, please. Colleen Kelly to the office."

For a few seconds, I sat very still, acutely aware that most of the kids toward the front of the room had turned in their seats to stare at me.

"Oh oh," I heard someone say, and then there was a sprinkling of laughter.

Being called to the office for some kids meant nothing but bad. But only twice before in my life had I been called to the school office. Once, when at the last minute, Mom, Dad, Rory, and Grandpa Shawn decided to attend the newspaper convention in Honolulu.

The second time the box called my name was when Nora was given tickets to a matinee in the city that day and asked me to come.

Sure, it's probably something like that, I thought as I left the classroom and hurried down the quiet hall toward the office. Something unexpected, something too good to miss. *Whatever it was, I'm game,* I decided. For the first time in a long time, I was in a carefree mood — hopeful. I wasn't even letting myself think about Jonathan today.

The office was empty except for a secretary typing at a desk in the back of the room. The assistant principal, Mrs. Chasan, sat at the front desk. She handed me the phone.

"For you, Colleen. It's your father."

Just before I put the receiver to my ear and before I said "Hello," I noticed Mrs. Chasan's eyes. Funny, I never noticed it before. I always thought of her as laughing, cheerful, but now I noticed: Mrs. Chasan had the saddest eyes in the world.

I understood why a second or two later. I understood the instant I heard Dad's voice. "Your mother's at the hospital with your grandfather, Colleen. I'm coming to school to pick you up right away. Bad news, sweetheart. Another heart attack — a bad one this time.

"It's very serious, I'm afraid," Dad said, hesitating, waiting for me to say something.

But I couldn't ask. I knew, but I didn't want him to say it. I felt Mrs. Chasan's arm around me, steadying me, holding me up.

Finally Dad said, "I'll be there in just a few minutes. Hold on, honey."

I sat on the couch waiting, and Mrs. Chasan sat with me, not saying very much, because, what could she say? I was glad she didn't talk, because then I didn't have to.

I didn't want to think either, but thoughts came anyway, and a memory. Grandpa Shawn (was it only last night?) saying: "Don't hurry, Colleen. I've got all the time in the world."

Then I had another memory right after that. A picture of him, standing there beside his desk just inside the circle of light, standing quite still watching me as I said good night. "Talk to you some more tomorrow, okay?"

He hadn't said yes or no. I remembered now he just stood there and smiled and blew me a kiss.

He was dead. I knew it — Grandpa Shawn was dead.

I knew it the minute I heard Dad's voice. I knew the hospital couldn't help him now, not all the machines in Intensive Care, not Dr. Prine, not all the starchy Miss Crisp nurses in the world.

Grandpa Shawn was dead.

I would never have a chance to tell him all the things I was too sleepy to tell him last night. And no more hugs, no more kisses (two for the pinkie). He was gone. If I climbed the stairs to the third floor, he wouldn't be there.

Grandpa Shawn was dead.

The days after Monday passed in a blur. Sometimes, I felt like I was standing off to one side, watching myself and everyone else rushing around, talking, making arrangements. So many arrangements: calls to make, people to see, things to do.

There were people to open the door to, flowers to order, guests to feed, to bring a drink or a cup of coffee to; people every hour of the day standing around, talking, even joking, talking about their kids, the weather, the price of food and gas, and sometimes about Grandpa Shawn. "A wonderful man, Shawn Kelly," all of them said.

I saw Maureen and Nora cry and Dad wept often, and once Rory came out of the bathroom with his eyes all red and bloodshot. I never caught Mom crying, though, or Patrick, and I . . . well . . . I *couldn't* cry. I was numb.

The wonderful numbness lasted all through the hours of the wake. It kept me calm and straight as I stood beside Patrick and greeted Grandpa Shawn's friends and colleagues and all the relatives. I didn't mind looking at Grandpa Shawn, or kneeling there in front of his coffin, because it wasn't real, not yet. Lying there, he didn't look very much different than he had a few nights before when I watched him at his desk.

He had told me he had all the time in the world. He had lied to me.

Somewhere, right in the center of my numbness, I felt a sharp pinch, and then another one. It hurt. I had to get out of the softly lit, flower-filled room where Grandpa Shawn lay with his eyes closed.

I didn't say a word to anyone, just left the room, found my coat, and slipped past a group of strangers standing by the door. Outside, in the cold night air, I took a deep breath. Now I did feel real. I felt like me again. I would explain to Mom and Dad why I hadn't stayed until the end.

"Colleen?"

Jonathan's voice. I didn't want to see Jonathan now.

"I thought I saw you leave. I was going to wait until it was . . ."

He was standing very close to me.

"I didn't see you in there," I said. *So what if he was*, I thought. *What does it matter?*

"I waited for you after school Monday, then I called. Your sister Nora told me what happened. I'm so sorry, Colleen."

"I know — thank you."

"I called you, and I came over once. Colleen, are you okay? Can I help? I know how you feel. I felt the same way about Grandma Holmes."

He *didn't* know how I felt. How could he? The way I loved Grandpa Shawn was special. *No one* could know how I felt.

"Let me drive you home now, Colleen. Just stay here for a minute until I let someone know I'm taking you."

"No," I said. It sounded loud in the October night. He turned back to me.

"No? Why not, Colleen? I really want to talk to you."

"Not tonight," I said. "I just can't tonight."

"Colleen . . ." His voice was breaking. *Of course*, I thought. *Everyone else can cry and let their voices break.*

"No," I said, "I have to go home now." *I sound like a whiny little girl,* I thought vaguely.

I hurried away, found Patrick's car in the parking lot, and let myself in. I sat there looking out the window, watching the lights along Main Street. In a little while, I saw Mom and Maureen and knew it must be after ten. On the porch of the huge white funeral home I saw Patrick standing under the light, talking with Jonathan. Their heads were close together, Patrick's fox-red hair shining, and Jonathan's glossy hair, satin-black under the light. Patrick was talking hard, I could tell. His arms were going like mad the way they do when he's upset. I wondered what he could be saying, but when he finally came and found me waiting for him in his car, he didn't tell me, and I didn't ask him.

On the way home, I was glad that Patrick didn't try to make conversation. In my mind I was seeing quite clearly a large room paneled in warm oak, a cozy room but definitely elegant. I very distinctly saw the rug: friendly blue dragons resting in a cream and apricot, blue-edged sea. There was a large oil painting hanging above the mantel. The painting was the only thing in the room I couldn't see very clearly.

But of course I knew who it would be. In time.

Chapter 17

"*J*onathan was just here," Nora said, coming into our bedroom. "I asked him to come in, but he wouldn't. He said, 'Tell Colleen to meet me at Hagan's. I have something important to tell her.' Then he got in his cute little car and drove away. Colleen, what's *with* you two anyway?"

What could be so important? Was he going away? Had he decided Springwood just didn't make it next to London or Zurich? Maybe he just wanted to tell me off, tell me I was much too moody, much too difficult, so let's forget it and just be friends.

"Listen, Colleen," Nora said. "I know you hate personal questions, but do you love Jonathan? I mean, Colleen, do you really care about the guy? Because if you do, I think you better get over there. He looks terrible."

"*How* terrible?" I asked quickly. "What do you mean?"

"Ah," she said. "So you do love him. I gotcha!"

I looked at her hard. "Nora, was that just a trick to find out my business."

She looked hurt. "No, honeybun, it wasn't. Jonathan doesn't look good. He looks like he hasn't slept in days. Last Sunday when he was over, he looked super. I was impressed. We were all impressed. This morning he looks like an unmade bed! Hair going every which way, a ratty old sweater, old jeans with mud on the knees. I mean, he didn't look preppie today. He reminded me of Dad after he's spent a hard day in his garden."

For some reason I was annoyed. "So what's wrong with that? There's nothing wrong with a little clean mud? Have you got something against dirt?"

Nora and Mrs. Holmes, birds of a feather.

Nora was grinning. "Colleen to the defense, huh? Gotcha again. You really *do* love him."

I shrugged and began to make my bed. It was about time. It had to be after eleven o'clock. Usually on Saturdays, I'm up early. I have no choice. Maureen and Nora are early birds, bouncing around the room, chattering away at the crack of dawn. Today, either they had been very quiet or I had been extra tired. I slept until after ten, washed and dressed, and sat back down on my bed. I was restless, but I hadn't been able to decide what to do with the day.

"I suppose I should go," I said, half to myself. "I guess he wouldn't have come over if it wasn't important."

I finished my bed and went over to the front window and looked out.

I missed Grandpa Shawn so much. It was strange. Everyone in the house had said the same thing, he really hadn't spent that much time downstairs with the family, but somehow he was able to make his presence felt anyway. Rory said, "I guess it was just knowing he could come down the stairs at any minute and be part of us."

I knew what he meant. For me, the hardest part was knowing I couldn't go up the stairs and be part of him, his world. So far, I hadn't been able to go near his room. I just didn't think I could *stand* it.

Nora was sitting cross-legged on the floor in front of her huge ballet mirror. She had pulled her hair back with a rubber band in a crude pony tail, and now she was dotting her face with a magic marker.

I went and stood behind her and put my hands on my hips. "Nora, what are you doing?"

Sometimes I couldn't believe my sister.

She grinned and kept dotting. "We have a new director — really a darling guy. His name is Lance Girado. Don't you love it? Anyway, he mentioned a part which calls for a redhead with freckles, kind of a country bumpkin type. I told him I was perfect, with my hair and all, but he just shook his head and said, "No, dear — you're much too pretty. Isn't that awful? I want to show him he's wrong, not only because I want the part, but because I think I'm . . . well, I may be in love with him."

I had to laugh. "It's awful because he thinks you're pretty?"

"Well, no," she admitted. "I suppose not. So you think I should forget freckles, Colleen?"

I opened the closet and searched for my riding boots and found them hiding under what looked like a cape that had been custom-made for Count Dracula — black velvet with a high, stiff collar.

"Well?" Nora was waiting for my answer.

"Not green freckles anyway," I said, pulling on my boots. "Nora, does that stuff wash off?"

Her eyes widened. "Good heavens, I hope so. Lance is picking me up in about twenty minutes! We're having lunch at The Harlequin."

She wiped frantically at the dots on her face. "I didn't notice I was doing them green. Why didn't you tell me?"

"Sorry," I said. "You have fun with Lance. I'm going over to Hagan's."

"Oh, no, you're not!"

I turned in the doorway.

"Come over here, honeybun — take a look. And you think green dots are bad? If Jonathan looked like an unmade bed, you look like a sleeping bag after a camping trip. Didn't you plan to brush your hair this morning? Sometimes I wonder about you. You've got the best hair in the house, the best features, and you don't do a thing with yourself. Maureen and I both could strangle you sometimes — that perfect nose Great-Grandma gave only to you, the perfect everything. If you weren't our sister, if we didn't love you, we'd hate your guts."

She had to be kidding! Maureen and Nora envious of my looks?

"Close your mouth, love, you'll let in all the flies. Come here to Nora and let me fix you. Someday I'm going to get you in my clutches and do something with you. Do some eyes maybe, and some warm blush."

I stood very still while she brushed my hair. "Okay," I said, feeling suddenly shy and shaky. I didn't want her to see the tears in my eyes, so I said, "Just no green freckles, please, okay?"

" 'Course not," she said. "There, now you look better, ready to face your public. After all, Colleen, you have an image to live up to. *You're a Kelly.*"

She was getting theatrical now, but she couldn't have said anything more wonderful: "You're a Kelly." And she certainly couldn't know what it meant to me. Impulsively, still feeling kind of shy, I hugged her.

"Thanks, Nora," I said. "For everything."

She was scrubbing at her dots again.

"That's all right, love — anytime."

When I got to Hagan's, Jonathan wasn't there. His car was, though, and Black Satin's stall was empty. J. J. was in the barn, helped me saddle Samson, and told me Jonathan had left a message. He would meet me at Squirrel Brook.

J. J. sighed, and jammed his hands in his back pockets. "I wish I was like Jonathan," he said. "I guess he always says and does the right thing — otherwise, you wouldn't love him, right? Mom says Jonathan Holmes is a perfect gentleman. She thinks you and Jonathan make a wonderful couple."

I couldn't answer him right away. I was thinking about how both Nora and now J. J. believed I was in love with Jonathan. I thought, too, of what J. J. had just said about Jonathan always saying or doing the right thing. J. J. could believe that because he really didn't know Jonathan at all. He looked up to him as a hero, someone to be like. He could only see what he wanted to see.

And what about me? Wasn't that what I had done? Hadn't I selected only parts of Jonathan to love? His soft voice, his sensitivity, his elegance. The other parts, the parts of Jonathan I didn't want, I threw out. As Dad would say: ". . . throwing out the baby with the bathwater."

Jonathan stood on the bank of Squirrel Brook, hands jammed in his back pockets, hair tousled, an anxious what-should-I-do look in his eyes.

I dismounted and gave Samson a push toward the thicket where Jonathan's Thoroughbred stood free.

I didn't tie Samson either. "Go see Black Satin," I said. "She's going to be so happy."

Jonathan was waiting for me, too, but he didn't seem very happy. One look at his eyes, the expression on his face, the down-droop of his mouth, told me he was very upset, *miserable.* I knew the feeling.

I walked over and stood beside him. I didn't say anything at first, and neither did he. We both just looked into the brook and at a new wood sculpture in the water: five or six medium size trees criss-crossed in the center of the brook, their trunks sharpened like pencils. The beavers had done it again.

"Amazing," I said. "Hey, aren't you freezing?"

I know I was glad I had my wool checked shirt on over my sweater. Jonathan's sweater, as well as being ratty as Nora had said, was very thin, definitely not something meant for an almost November day in the woods.

He glanced down at himself and shrugged. I could tell it didn't matter very much. "I was in the garden, and then I was in the car. I just took off, I didn't really think."

He looked at me and then away. He stared down at the water. "I had to see you, Colleen. I couldn't stand it anymore. Your brother said to give you time, not to bother you. He said you must have a pretty good reason not to want to see me or even talk to me on the phone. Patrick told me: 'I like you, pal, but I love my sister. No one better hurt her.'"

Maybe my brother's macho act the Sunday just before Jonathan came for dinner wasn't an act at all. I hadn't realized I had such a fierce protector. Plus now I knew what had Patrick's arms flapping like a windmill the night of Grandpa Shawn's wake.

Jonathan still didn't look up. "Colleen, I have to know what I did, so at least I know what to apologize for. Know what not to do anymore.

What did I do? I've been beating my brains out all week and I still don't know."

"Jonathan," I said soothingly. He really was upset. "Take it easy, calm down. Don't get so excited. You didn't . . ."

He wasn't listening. "I am upset, damn it. How can I not be when the girl I'm in love with suddenly won't even talk to me, the same girl who said she loved me. Tell me — *what did I do wrong?*"

I took a couple steps toward him, close enough to touch, and then for something to do, because I wasn't very sure of myself now, I began picking off, one by one, the little nubbles of wool on his sweater.

"You and Dad," I said softly. "Two of a kind — green thumbs and pilly sweaters. Except his is bright red and yours is . . ."

"Dirty blue. I guess I look terrible, huh?"

"Nora said you did. She said you looked like an unmade bed."

I stole a look at him. He didn't know whether to laugh or be insulted. "She did, did she?"

He ran one hand nervously through his dark hair. I reached into my shirt-jacket pocket and took out my pink pocket comb.

"Here, bend down a little," I said. "Let me do it. I don't want you tearing your hair out over me, or beating your brains out either. I like your hair, I like your brains."

He didn't say a word, but he bent his head obediently and I stood on tiptoes. I combed his hair very carefully, one strand at a time and watched it slowly settle back into the good shape I was used to, satiny again, neat. Now that his hair was in place he looked much better, more like Jonathan.

Then I stopped, hand and comb and arm frozen in midair.

Wrong! Absolutely wrong!

Hair combed, hair uncombed — Jonathan.

Soft laugh, idiot laugh — Jonathan.

Fashionable, ratty — still Jonathan.

Quiet, rowdy, shy, superconfident — *all Jonathan!*

Suddenly, almost throwing him off balance, I reached up, and with both hands I messed up his hair. I did a great job of it, too. When I finished, it was literally standing on end. I stood back and looked — and laughed.

"You're really cute, you know that, preppie?" I said.

He was laughing, too, but not very much. "What was that all about? Are you crazy or something?"

He looked so bewildered I had to feel sorry for him. I realized I was way ahead of him. I knew what I was going to do, and he didn't.

I moved even closer until I could hear every breath he took, and then I stood on tiptoes again and wound my arms around his neck. I gave him one quick little kiss on the mouth, and then I leaned my head back so I could see his face.

"Jonathan," I whispered. "You didn't do anything wrong. I'm the one who should apologize. I just had everything confused for a while. I don't anymore."

He was wary. "I don't understand."

"Sometime I'll explain," I told him. "I really don't want to go into it now. I just want you to know I figured things out."

His eyes were soft now, and I felt his arms around me. "You're okay now?"

I nodded and tried to smile. "I always was. I just didn't know it."

He didn't answer, just hugged me tighter.

"I still hurt a lot," I said. "I miss my grandfather. We were very close."

"I know about that," Jonathan said tenderly. "Your sister Maureen told me. She said, 'Grandpa Shawn and Colleen are so much alike, that's probably why they got along so well!'"

I was surprised. Maureen said that? I would have to think about that later.

"Colleen? What I was going to tell you . . . what I was going to say, no matter what happened . . ."

He hesitated, his eyes closed.

"The something important?" I prompted.

He nodded and opened his eyes, and now he stared at my mouth. "I just wanted to tell you . . ."

"Yes, Jonathan?"

"I love you. I really love you."

I didn't have a chance to say "I love you, too" until three fantastic kisses later. There was no real hurry, of course, but I *did* say it.

Chapter 18

I was vacuuming our bedroom and put the vacuum down for the fifty-eighth time. How can you vacuum properly where every sixth inch of floor space is booby-trapped with barrettes, pennies, a package of false fingernails, a pair of manicure scissors, and shoes—scads of shoes, slippers, sneakers, high heels. Couldn't Nora and Maureen ever learn to put their things away?

Mom was sitting on Nora's bed watching me and laughing. Mom's eyes scanned the bedroom and then her gaze rested on me. I thought I detected a glint of mischief in her eyes.

"Darling," Mom said finally. "How would you like to get away from all this? How would you like having your own room?"

My voice squeaked. "My own room?"

"The third floor," Mom said, almost breathing the words. "Your grandfather left it to you!"

"Left it to me?" Now my voice was merely a breath.

"He didn't add it to his will, Colleen, but in a way it's a very real part of his legacy. He said he was depending on us to see to it. Anyway, Grandpa Shawn's room is yours now."

She was smiling happily. "Everyone agrees it's a wonderful idea. Maureen and Nora especially. Maureen said you deserved a million dollars for putting up with their nonsense. Patrick said he thought you'd rather have the room than the money. Anyway, it was unanimous. We all agree it's the best gift he could have given you. We all know you need more privacy than the rest of us groupies. Just like your grandfather did. I want you to know we've always respected that in him, and we try very hard to do the same with you. Maureen says we don't always make it. She said she thinks you're a saint for not telling us off. But I told her I thought you understood that we can't help it, and that you allowed us our differences."

I didn't know what to say. Suddenly I felt very humble and shaky, too. I put my head down on Mom's shoulder.

"I'm not sure I can . . ." I whispered. "I haven't been able to go near, to go up there since . . ."

She stroked my hair. "I've got a confession to make," she said. "It took me until today before *I* could go up. But I made myself because I wanted to get it ready for you. I just this minute finished. I understand how you feel, Colleen. We all do. We miss him, too."

"I know," I whispered. I kept my head on her

shoulder, and we sat like that for a while without talking.

"One nice thing, though . . ." she said, finally breaking the silence.

"What?" I murmured, not quite listening. I was picturing the room upstairs, the blue chair, the oak desk.

"Cleaning his room — it was so easy. Your grandfather was a tidy, thoughtful man, like you. Except I did find . . ."

I heard the smile in her voice and I looked up at her. There were tears in her eyes.

". . . some empty soda cans, and a bag of potato chips — half-full."

She stood up then, just stood there very still, her chin up, blinking her eyes like mad. She gave me a misty smile and left the room.

I felt very close to Mom and even a lot like her. At least we were alike in our feelings, our sorrow. And I thought about how she had made that first, sad climb to the third floor. For me. Mom did it for me, because she loved me.

Finally, I made myself get up and finish the vacuuming. Then I went to take my shower. I had promised Jonathan I'd be ready to go riding with him at noon, and I didn't want to keep him waiting.

Chapter 19

*W*hen Jonathan and I got to our favorite spot, Squirrel Brook, we dismounted and let Black Satin and Samson visit while we sat on a fat old log and held hands. Finally, with his free hand, Jonathan reached in his shirt pocket and handed me a tiny, gift-wrapped box.

"Ohhh, Jonathan," I breathed.

He grinned and let go of my hand. "I'll give you two minutes to open it, and then I want your hand back."

I laughed and pulled at the yellow ribbon. "It's not my birthday or anything," I said.

His smile was warm and his voice very soft. "I saw this and I knew it had to be yours. It *is* you."

I lifted the lid from the little white box, and then the layer of cotton. There nestled on a bed of white was an enameled violet, so detailed and delicately shaded, it seemed like a real flower. It was attached to the thinnest of gold chains. It was beautiful.

"It's beautiful, Jonathan," I said, looking at

him, not ashamed of the tears that suddenly filled my eyes.

He was pleased. "So are you, Colleen," he said. "Let me help you put it on."

He fumbled with the clasp for a few minutes, but finally the violet lay against the creamy wool of my sweater. I looked down at it, admiring it, and then he picked up my hand again and squeezed it.

Jonathan looked at the violet and then at me. "That's so you won't forget your friend here with the green thumb."

"You *are* my friend, Jonathan," I said seriously. "Not just a boyfriend either. I think you're the only person in the world who understands me now that Grandpa Shawn is gone."

He shook his head emphatically. "Not true, Colleen. You forgot about your sisters, Patrick, your dad — everyone in your wonderful family. They all understand you. After you went to bed that Sunday when I was over, when we were playing cards, I got the whole scoop on you."

He smiled. "Know what Rory said you were?"

Here we go, I thought — Little Miss Mimosa Tree. But I was wrong.

"Rory said: 'Colleen is our rare treasure.' Maureen and Nora both said you were 'very special.' In fact, that's the word they all kept using when they talked about you. I got the impression they thought of themselves as cotton, and you and your Grandpa Shawn as silk. I think I already told you Maureen said you and your Grandfather were two of a kind."

Then he lowered his head and I couldn't see his eyes, and his next two words were indistinct, muffled by the wool of his sweater.

I bent my own head and rested my cheek against his. "What did you say?" I asked.

"I said, you don't know how lucky you are."

"Lucky, Jonathan?"

His chin lifted and he looked me squarely in the eye. His eyes were smoky dark, almost angry. "Yes, lucky. I guess all my life I would have given anything to be part of such a great family, to have people of my own who were really interested in me — understood me, loved me, wanted me around."

The last three words had a jagged sound, as if they had hurt coming out of him. I thought of Mr. and Mrs. Holmes and the beautiful, quiet house on the lake, and the way Jonathan's face changed when he entered that house. It occurred to me then that no one really wanted the quietness. It was just that they didn't have anything to say to each other. It occurred to me too that Jonathan was, and always had been, lonely, and that he had never felt special in his life.

But I didn't tell him these thoughts. Instead I told him how Mom had said: "Jonathan's terrific — you have good taste," and how Nora had known and understood about my loving him.

"Hey, Jonathan," I said. "Think you can get out of Sunday dinner at your house, and come to mine instead? No problem — set another place, that's all. We do it all the time — standard Kelly procedure."

Had I really said that? *We* do it all the time? Amazing! I really did feel like a Kelly now. One of them.

I tugged at his hand. "Come on, Jonathan," I said. "Let's go to my house now. I'm getting kind of cold and I can just picture one of Rory's famous fires blazing in the family room. Of course, you'll probably get roped into bringing more wood in. That's one of the prices you'll pay for making my family like you so much. They'll just assume you're one of the family. Anyway, let's go now and see what's happening."

"You mean it, Colleen? You don't think they'll mind?"

Here was the shy, unsure-of-himself Jonathan again. My heart was almost bursting with love for him.

"Mind?" I said indignantly. "Jonathan, in our house people come first."

All the way home, I kept hearing the word Jonathan had told me my family used when they had talked about me — special. They thought I was special. And I knew, "special" is a far cry from "misfit" or "oddball." Special is what Grandpa Shawn was. In that case, special isn't a bad thing to be. Not bad at all.

I looked at him and then I put one finger against his mouth. "People come first in our hearts, too," I whispered. "My heart especially. I love you, Jonathan."

We didn't kiss. We didn't need to. The look that passed between us then was better than any kiss — ever.